GHOST EYES

S.J. GARRETT

This book is a work of fiction. Names, characters, places, and incidents are the product of the author's imagination or are used fictitiously. Any resemblance to actual events, locales, or persons, living or dead, is coincidental.

GHOST EYES Copyright ©2016
Line By Lion Publications
318 Louis Coleman Jr. Dr.
Louisville, KY 40212
www.linebylion.com

ISBN: 978-1-940938-68-4

Prologue

"Her Royal Highness, the Crown Princess Gardina de Coronia of the Campbell Royal Family."

Standing in the shadows near the doors, the white haired young woman grimaced mentally. She hated that title almost as much as she hated the thick and voluminous gold dress she was wearing. It was Coronia, and it was smothering hot. Well, at least *this* portion of the country was smothering hot.

Coronia was a country caught like a wedge in between the other two countries that made up the largest landmass of the world of Iria. Rikan and Desertia, the other two countries, were both larger than Coronia, and they were also much hotter and much drier in places. Desertia was in possession of the Greater Water Runic; because of it, they were able to keep most of their country lush and green. The heat, well, that couldn't be helped.

All three countries, and all three kingdoms, were each in possession of a Greater Runic. Gardina wasn't even sure which Runic her kingdom was supposed to have. It had been lost before her birth. Regardless, it was her rightful possession should it ever be located again. No one else would ever be able to use it.

"Gardina!" her younger sister hissed. "Go in! They're waiting!"

She took a deep breath. "I'm going, Rose," she muttered. "I'm going." She straightened her shoulders and shook back her long white hair. With regal dignity, she walked into the throne room. Everyone present bowed or curtsied elegantly as she passed and it formed a long wave across the room.

When she was before the throne, she curtsied to her mother and father gracefully. "You sent for me?" she asked.

"Naturally." Her mother smiled and gestured to the handsome young man standing just to the side. "Your fiancé has arrived for the final preparations for the wedding."

"I look forward to it," Prince Leonasis said as he walked forward and took Gardina's hand. "I will be quite honored to claim you for my wife."

Gardina knew it was a sound match, and she liked Leo well enough, but as he leaned down to lightly kiss her, she wondered why the hell she was so reluctant to marry him. Something about the way he smelled, of all things, seemed entirely wrong to her.

Two hours later, she was in her bedroom and stripping off her dress as fast as Humanly possible. She didn't care if it complimented her slender figure. She didn't care that it matched her pale gold eyes. She *did* care that it was making her feel as if she was going to pass out. The dainty qualities were her sister's specialty. She was the sturdy one.

As she flopped down on her bed in nothing but her silk slip, she contemplated the tapestry on the wall that fancifully depicted the Evermore and the two who called it home.

Like all creatures on Iria, she believed in the afterlife realm known as the Evermore. It was the place where all spirits went to when they died. It was there, in that place, that the goddess and god of the world resided. Sometimes they were called Moon and Sun. Most of the time it was Light and Dark. No matter their names, they were two and they were one.

"Well," she decided as she sat up again, "at least if you're going to die, there's somewhere really nice to go to. I wonder if the Etyrnals feel cheated in any way. They're immortal, so they'll never go to Evermore. Then again . . . Light and Dark *do* act as their guardians so . . ."

She sighed. "Stop talking to yourself. Damn it, I need to get a cat or something." She got to her feet and went over to her closet to pull out a light summer dress in pale blue. All her clothes, she noted with some amusement, were pale. She supposed it was because her skin was so fair as to nearly be translucent. Dark colors just washed her out.

Her day was a busy one as always. It consisted of more training for the duties she would be assuming when she took the throne as queen. That event would occur within a month of her marriage. She was twenty years old already; there was no need to wait for her to reach the proper age.

She was due to have dinner with her fiancé in the little cottage he was using while he visited. Deciding to see if a little fun and excitement was what they needed to strike any sort of sparks, she set out early toward the cottage, hoping to get there before he did and surprise him.

As she walked, she thought back over how long she had known Leo. He was a prince from Rikan, one of three in fact, and he wasn't set to inherit since he wasn't the eldest. She wouldn't admit it out loud, but she did have a preference for his eldest brother. Pity he was madly in love with his own fiancée. Then again, that was probably why she liked him. He turned into an adorable sweetheart around his ladylove.

The cottage had a light on near the back and that startled her. She could have sworn Leo was out seeing the town and greeting the people. Her stomach began to dip even as her heart quivered. Something told her she wasn't going to like whatever she was about to see.

Steeling herself, she walked over and opened the door quietly to peer around the edge. Shock lasted only a moment before being drowned by a wave of searing anger. She shut the door just as quietly and turned around to go back toward the palace. At the least, she finally knew why his scent smelled wrong to her.

She went immediately to the throne room where her mother and father were holding court. There were several courtiers present but she didn't care. "Mother, Father, may I have a word?" she asked.

"Certainly." Her mother frowned as she clearly saw the signs of her oldest daughter's fury. "What's wrong, darling? Do you want some privacy?"

"Oh no." Her smile was tight-lipped. "For all I know, some of the people here are already aware." She crossed her arms. "I request the right to dissolve my engagement to Leonasis on the grounds of adultery before marriage."

Shocked silence fell. Her father's eyes slowly widened. "Are you sure?"

"When I walk into his cottage to find him with his pants down and very happily copulating with a servant, I can say with one hundred percent certainty that I am sure." Her pale gold eyes were like shards of glass. "I don't *care* if it was 'just a servant'. I will not marry a man I cannot trust to be faithful to me."

"Indeed you will not!" he almost roared as he got to his feet. "Guards!" he barked. "Fetch Leonasis! And make sure his pants are on!"

Ten minutes later, a very shame faced Leo was escorted by five guards into the throne room. Gardina was standing to one side with her sister, and Leo tried to send her a pleading look. She merely narrowed a scathing look on him before turning her back dismissively.

"What is the meaning of this, Prince Leonasis?" the queen asked icily. "You were cheating on Gardina?"

"It was before we were wed!" he tried to protest. "What difference does it make? It didn't mean anything!"

Gardina turned toward him. "You know what?

That makes it even worse. If you had told me you were madly in love with her, but knew her station would keep you apart, I might have forgiven you. In fact, I would have cheerfully found a way to help you get together."

"Gardina, please," he pleaded. "If I return home this way, I will be disgraced!"

"The same way you have disgraced me?" she retorted sharply. "I played the fool, thinking you cared for me. I should have followed my gut the minute I realized how you smelled." He stared at her in confusion and she bit out, "You smell like women's perfume. If you're fooling around enough to absorb the scent, then you're worse than an alley cat!"

She turned on her heel with regal dignity and swept from the room. Her sister Rose followed closely behind. "Gardina," she whispered, "I'm so sorry."

"Don't be." Gardina found a smile. Her baby sister was five years younger but they got along like best friends as much as sisters. "I'm still young. I have time to find someone worth loving."

Leo was allowed to remain on palace grounds for the night, but he would be escorted home the next day. Notice was already being sent to his father, and there was no one who doubted he would be just as disgusted as the Coronia Kingdom. Gardina was beloved by all who met her, and they did not want to see her hurt.

It was close to midnight when Gardina realized she couldn't sleep. Since Coronia was located along the northern edge of the country, the castle itself was situated along the edge of the ocean. In desperate need of some thinking time, she slipped out of the palace and headed down to the cliffs that overlooked the ocean.

There was a large rock on the edge that she sat down on. As she stared across the top of the dark waves, she told herself that she needed to look on the bright side. At least she had found out about Leo's infidelity before they were married rather than after. She had no idea where he had been, and she really didn't *want* to know.

There was a sound behind her and she stood swiftly to turn around. Much to her shock, she saw Leo charging toward her from the trees with a look of rage on his face. A sword was in his hands. "You've destroyed me!" he screamed at her. "I'll kill you!"

She took a step back in reflex and her foot went off the edge of the cliff. Shock froze her voice as she found herself falling through the air. Her life was going to end like this? She wasn't going to get to kick his butt for even daring to come after her? She was going to have a word with Light and Dark when she reached Evermore; that was certain.

The impact with the ocean was like hitting solid stone. It broke every bone in her body and drove all air from her lungs. As she sank under the waves, her consciousness was aware that she was dead. She was drifting . . . drifting . . . soon she would be in Evermore.

She touched the bottom of the ocean and her hand brushed against an odd shaped stone. It began to glow with gray light and suddenly shot at her. Even her consciousness felt pain then as the odd stone began to force its way inside her body. Then, suddenly, everything was black. There was no pain. No life. There was nothing. There was no Evermore. There wasn't a goddess or a god. There was . . . nothing.

She had been cheated. In that moment, Gardina stopped believing.

She opened her eyes to find herself staring up at the canopy of trees over her head. She knew exactly where she was located. She was in one of the forests of Coronia. She cautiously sat up with a hand pressed her heart. Her first reaction was sheer shock. How was she alive? She had to be alive; she had a body. Ghosts didn't have bodies.

She felt a throbbing under her hand and staggered to her feet to go stare in the river beside her. Clearly etched into her chest was the mark of a Runic: the Greater Ghost Runic. It was the only Runic born from the Ghost Moon, the only moon of the thirteen in the sky that was gray.

"So then I'm alive?" she whispered to herself, her hand covering the mark.

"Oh no," a woman's voice said calmly behind her. "You're quite dead as well, fledgling. Technically one might say you're both, but, well, that's so much more complicated. For now, we'll just say you're dead."

She felt an absurd urge to laugh. "Oh, well, that's alright then."

Chapter One

(Year 3155, Rikan, Deserted Woods)

It was another waking dream. She had grown used to them over the last three centuries and had, in fact, come to rely on them. They kept her sane amid an insane world.

They always started the same way. Her sight turned to a soft silvery color with everything fading into light. Shadows whispered and teased the edges of her vision. Hands behind her back, Gardina continued to move down the path she was traversing and felt darkness close behind her protectively.

The soft and welcoming feeling of coming home effused her soul. Even as she became conscious of it, she became conscious of the slender woman now walking beside her. "War," she said.

The silver haired woman inclined her head slightly. She was of only slightly taller height than Gardina, but Gardina was shorter than average. If Gardina envied anything of her ethereal, Etyrnal companion, it was that her figure looked so lush and beautiful. As generous as love, and as giving as life. "Inevitable," the woman said softly, and her voice was as mystical as life itself.

"Is it always?" She linked her hands behind her

back and let her feet leave the ground so that she was floating along.

"I have never believed any race is inevitably drawn to war," the woman decided after a moment. "But dominant creatures want to dominate. If they are pitted to another dominant creature, fighting will ensue. Sometimes verbally. Sometimes physically. Humans, Fae, Etyrnals . . . they are no different from animals in that. But their methods of domination can be infinitely more brutal."

"What of evil?"

"Ah, always the wild card." She made a gesture with a slender and curiously strong hand. "When evil arrives, then things certainly change. Domination is no longer the game. Destruction is." She turned her gaze to the distant horizon where the sun slowly rose. "You have sensed it, little ghost?"

"Mmm. Hard not to." Her delicate ears detected the sound of the far away battles raging even though they were more than two days' distance from her current location. Perhaps what she heard was not the fighting, but the death. Every soul screaming as life ended before it wanted. "All this blood over a piece of pretty glass."

The woman slid a smiling look at her. "You still do not believe in the Evermore? Or in Light and Dark? You do not believe that the moons wept with joy when life came forth and thus cried the items we call Greater Runics and Lesser Runics?"

"I believe it about as much as I believe there's a good Fae who likes to deliver presents to children every harvest festival." Gardina lightly touched the gray tribal mark burned into the skin between her breasts. "I know these came of the moons. But they're just little shards. Not tears."

"Then what of me?"

"A figment of my imagination. The spirit of my Runic maybe. I have stopped asking. If I have imagined you, then I don't wish to know. Our conversations help me stay stable when I wonder if I'm being ripped apart."

"Such a contradiction you are." The words were warm and teasing. The kiss she brushed over Gardina's forehead was loving and motherly. "Truly you are Gray." She began to dissolve into little ribbons of silvery-green. "My little ghost."

In moments, Gardina was alone. The scenery returned to normal and the darkness of night settled in around her. The sun continued to rise in the distance and the voices of the trapped dead cried in her ears. One voice sounded particularly loud, and unlike the rest of them, it did not belong.

She rose higher in the air as she began to dissolve into the mists of morning. She was the Ghost Hunter. Her duty was to banish lingering spirits who needed to go, and call back spirits that needed to stay. Such was the curse of her immortal life.

Such was the curse of her undead existence.

(Desertia, Scorching Sands)

It wasn't the heat.

It was the humanity.

A bloody war raged outside his tent. The air was dry and dusty, and if a wind blew, it blew only hot air. The air was as dead as the bodies lying across the battlefield. Even inside the sheltering tents, there was no relief. The air smelled of death. The heat suffocated. And the war kept raging.

Sweat slid down the commanding officer's back under his tunic. He had removed his armor to escape the oppressive heat, but he knew that when he put the armor on again that he would burn his hands. Nothing gathered heat as well as metal in the desert.

He had stopped pacing the confines of his tent because the exertion was smothering, yet sitting at his desk brought no relief. If the Evermore had a hell, this was probably it.

It was enemy land. They knew this land. They were adapted to this land. On a curse, Matthias Logan shoved once more to his feet and began to pace off his frustration. Why was the Rikan Army even there? All this over those ridiculous bits of glass known as Greater Runics. Were they even as powerful as rumor claimed? He doubted it.

Only three Greater Runics were even known of, and of them, all had disappeared. About three centuries before, the Ghost Runic had disappeared from Coronia with the death of a monarch. Rikan had lost the Sovereign Runic in a bloody coup on the royal family almost thirty years earlier. Desertia claimed the Water Runic had disappeared as well, but few believed it. The land was, after all, still lush and green in the places they had cultivated over the centuries.

He was sick of the war. He was sick of losing good people. Watching the other side lose good people. What did he fight for? A greedy, sick old man who ruled a kingdom stained with blood? All the king wanted was to conquer more land and gain more power.

At the back of his mind echoed a soft mantra. It pulsed and beat over and over. The name of every soldier he had lost. If he closed his eyes, he saw weapons and magic tearing through flesh.

What if you left?

The soft, haunting voice whispered in his ears. He slowly sank down into his chair with his face pressed to his hands. The voice was feminine, innocent, and nearly child-like without belonging to a child. It was often there in his darkest moments. "I don't hear you," he murmured to himself.

Then why do you speak to me?

"I'm losing my mind."

A soft giggle echoed in his ears and then the voice was gone. But she had made her mark. He stared a bit blindly at the opening to his tent. What if he left? Why did he stay? "If I am to leave," he murmured softly, "give me some sort of sign."

The tent flap suddenly flew open and a young soldier rushed inside. His arms were wrapped fiercely around a small bloodstained child. "Commander!" he said urgently. "Innocent blood!"

Matthias felt a chill all the way to his soul. If there was any sanity among the insanity of war, it was that no innocent blood got spilled by anyone. "What happened?" he snapped as he got to his feet and crossed the tent. "How old is she?"

"She looks no more than four, but her family mark is dark enough that she ought to be older." The soldier shook from head to toe, his skin sickly. He swallowed hard. "She's from Desertia. S-she ran right into the battlefield and no one could call off the attacks in time. I told everyone she was dead and I was taking her body away. But I couldn't just . . ." His voice broke.

Matthias gently peeled down the edge of the ruined shirt the girl was wearing. The family mark on her upper arm was fading with her lifeforce, but it was distinct enough to place her age around seven. Family marks were what separated families into units. Marriage or adoption changed the mark but nothing else.

As always, he was conscious of the fact that he didn't *have* a family mark. He was the son of a servant from the former Rikan royal family, and in the coup, he had lost his family as well. His family mark had faded to nothingness with them. "Put her on the cot," he said quietly.

The soldier gently

put the girl down with shaking hands. "A baby," he whispered.

He was barely sixteen years old himself. Another insanity in the world to put war on the shoulders of the young. Matthias took a deep breath. He couldn't take the insanity anymore. He had asked for a sign. It had arrived. "I will tend to her," he said quietly. "If I can link my lifeforce to hers, I might be able to keep her alive long enough to find an accomplished healer. Return to your post."

The soldier hesitated. "Commander . . . we do not have any strong enough healers on our side."

"I know." Matthias met his eyes calmly.

After a pause, he slowly nodded as he understood. "I joined the army for you, Commander," he admitted quietly. "Because you are a good man and I believe you when you say that peace will someday come. You have my loyalty." With a sincere salute, he left the tent.

Matthias eased down onto the cot beside the girl. Linking his lifeforce to hers was a simple enough trick; anyone could do it even if they didn't have a Runic. All it meant was that he prevented her lifeforce from leaving and entering the realm of Evermore. If it did, her body would die.

He softly took one of her tiny hands in his. She was so outrageously delicate! She looked like a good wind would carry her away. Yet she was delicately lovely as well. If she lived, she would be breaking hearts someday; one of the gods had been practicing perfection when they made this little girl.

"Hey," he said softly, reaching for her with his lifeforce and using his voice as a focal point. "You're safe with me."

Her spirit fluttered against his and then latched on with a surprising strength. A little shiver went down his back. She was *powerful*. She would surely be a Runic Master someday. *Hey,* he thought again to her softly. The mind-to-mind communication was a natural byproduct of their linked lifeforces, and if maintained for long enough, would become permanent. *Can you hear me?*

Who are you?

He smiled. *I'm a friend. I'm trying to save your life if you'll let me.* He almost instantly felt the renewed surge of her will. She wouldn't go easily. *What's your name?*

Kaeleigh, but everyone calls me Kae. What's your name? Do you have a nickname? I can make you one if you want.

Utterly charmed, he linked their fingers as well. *My name is Matthias. Most call me 'Commander.'*

That isn't a name! It's a title. *And it's silly. I'm gonna call you by your name 'cause you're stuck with me now and you won't be alone anymore, okay?*

He gently brushed her hair out of her eyes. There were no secrets between those with linked lifeforces. She saw him as profoundly as he saw her. His eyes watched critically as her wounds were slowly covered by the soft blue-green color that meant his health was halting the loss of hers. *You're alone too, little one.*

Maybe. A little. But I wasn't alone when I got hurt. She was *there. She was sad. She frowned at me because I'm not supposed to die. I was scared. But she played her flute. It made me happy. Then suddenly you were there.*

His heart began to beat a little harder. *Who is she?*

She didn't say her name. But she smiled when she saw you. It made me happy.

"By the moons," he muttered. Did he really have a guardian spirit of some kind? He could have sworn only Etyrnals bonded to mortals. If she *was* an Etyrnal, how was she able to pass between day and night? He had heard her at both times.

Listen! She's playing again!

The excitement in Kae's voice instantly had his attention. He tuned out the sounds of the war beyond his tent and focused. The music came softly at first and then louder as he focused on it. Haunting and ethereal, the flute sounded as if it wept through the winds. Tears burned his eyes briefly. It seemed he and Kae weren't the only ones who felt alone.

Matt?

He immediately turned back. *What, Kae?*

If I don't die, what should I do? My family is gone. My brother died in the war yesterday. My mom and dad died a year ago.

He took a long breath. *You can stay with me, Kae. If you want to.*

Do you have a house?

Not yet.

Horses?

He smiled. *Potentially.*

Okay. Can I go to sleep now? I won't die. Promise.

Okay. Go to sleep. The soft hum of her presence promptly silenced in his mind. He let out a long breath as he released her hand. The link between them would remain without the physical contact.

Instead, he focused on wrapping and binding her wounds. She had lost far too much blood. He wasn't even sure an accomplished healer would help her. Only the Fae and Etyrnals had the potential to heal on this scale, but they were very solitary societies; finding someone would be challenging.

She slept away the rest of the afternoon. He continued on as if nothing had changed. He sent units into battle, listened to the reports of casualties, and tried to cling onto his sanity with his fingertips.

A particularly violent fire blast tore through a portion of his encampment. While soldiers scrambled to put out the flames, he found himself frozen with horror as he stared at the decimation. He could see the burning bodies of those who had not escaped. Their screams seared his ears.

He felt soft hands covering his eyes. His sight blurred and removed the macabre images from view. *Stop*, the feminine voice breathed in his ears. *Do not look, fledgling.* Pain echoed in her voice. *You are too young to view this.*

"Who are you?" he asked very softly. He did not shake off her presence though he knew there was no one there physically. "Are you an Etyrnal?"

Yes.

"Then I am your . . ." he tried to remember the word, "your Devoted?"

Seems so. Her soft breath seemed to touch his ear as she whispered, *Walk away, Matthias Logan. Walk away. Come to me. You are my Devotion. Bring Kae to me.*

He gave the slightest of nods before he turned and walked back into his tent. He wasn't entirely sure what it meant to be a Devoted, but he had heard that an Etyrnal could do no harm to theirs. They would, in fact, protect them until their Devoted died. If there was anyone he could trust, it was the mysterious Etyrnal who had kept him sane.

When night fell in the desert, the level of darkness was determined by how many moons were full. On that night there were four full moons, but all of them were Dark. The night was bathed in shadows more than light. Lamps lit throughout the camp to keep soldiers from running into objects and other people.

It was the red moon, the Sovereign Moon, that was highest in the sky when Matthias slipped from his tent with Kae in his arms. She was wide-awake but very quiet in his mind, conscious that he was doing something dangerous. Even dressed in black to blend in, he ran the risk of being seen.

He slipped along the edges of the camp until he reached the end. From there until the start of the forest a mile away, he would have no cover other than the night.

As he weighed his options, the night grew darker still as a storm slowly crept in. The moons were slowly obscured until it was so dark that even the lamps barely provided visibility. Sending thanks to whatever deity was aiding him, he slipped away from the camp and began to move across the chilly desert as fast as he could. Nights in the desert were as bitterly cold as the days were blistering hot.

The trees brought welcoming protection from the cold air when they reached them, and he felt only the slightest unease when the storm clouds passed and allowed light to filter into the forest so that he could see. He accepted that there were some beings who had powers beyond any mortal comprehension.

When dawn began to creep into the sky, he found shelter for himself and Kae in an underground cave. Tensely, he watched the sky from the entrance. As the first real rays moved over the horizon, he could hear the sudden distant explosions from his camp.

What did you do?

He filled the entrance with some boulders and then went back to Kae and wrapped his cloak more snugly around her. The cave was chilly without the sun to come inside. *I 'accidentally' left out some light sensitive weapons and Runics. They have adverse reactions to the sunlight just like Dark Etyrnals. Well, kind of. I've never heard of a Dark Etyrnal exploding.*

That would be messy. There was a pause, then she asked softly, *Do you know where to go?*

No, he admitted honestly. He smoothed her hair from her face. *But we'll get there eventually. Don't worry, Kae. Everything will be okay now.* He settled back against the wall and closed his eyes. He knew he would need his strength for the coming days. He didn't even know where he was going; he only knew that he was going to the Etyrnal who claimed him as her Devoted.

But . . . just what was a Devoted anyway?

Chapter Two

In her many long years, Gardina had seen the amazing feats a mortal body could accomplish when they were truly determined. She had seen a father be burned in a vicious fire and not even realize it until he had safely escorted his children to safety. She had seen a mere child take on a *nosferatu* with his bare hands and come away alive purely because the rogue hadn't been able to defend against the child's desperation.

She knelt beside the sleeping figure of Matthias and studied his face intently. It was not an unfamiliar face. Not anymore. From the moment she had laid eyes on him months before, she had felt the sharp compulsion to protect. Her Devotion. She hadn't thought she would ever have one.

Respect moved inside her as she tenderly brushed his hair from his eyes. He had walked without ceasing for nearly two days in his search for her. He had foregone sustenance in his determination to save Kae. Truthfully, she had not met a stronger willed person. He *lived*. His thirst for life rivaled that of an Etyrnal.

With a little sigh, she shook her head. Now

what the hell was she supposed to do? She had thought that an Etyrnal/Devoted relationship was supposed to be profound and comforting and uplifting. No one had bothered to tell her that she might be so deeply attracted to her Devoted. She was going to kick Selene. Hard.

But, well, she *was* still alive. Technically. Her body was more than functional in many ways. Desire was one of those ways, and it happily fluttered through her blood and the Runic that passed for her heart. Her fingers itched to get into his thick black hair and trace his stubborn mouth. He was gilded with gold from being in the sun too long, and his body was hard and powerful from a soldier's life.

"Oooh, damn it!" she muttered softly. She let her body go translucent to shed physical feelings but got a disappointment as she realized she *still* felt her blood heating at his presence. She was going to kick Selene and then she was going to kick Niall too!

Something stirred along the back of Matthias' mind. A touch as feminine as light and as fiercely protective as dark. A tender, cool touch brushed his cheek. His eyes instantly opened. And just as instantly, his heart stopped beating. He very nearly yelped, but hastily swallowed it. His eyes went wide.

The woman kneeling in front of him was so pale and ethereal that he was sure that he stared at a ghost. Thick white hair tumbled around her shoulders in a froth of curls and her pale gold eyes were soft and calming. Her skin was nearly cream in color, with only the faintest flush to give her a sense of life.

He could almost see through her, yet her body solidified and became real even as he watched. Little dimples crinkled at the corners of her eyes as she smiled at him. "Are you a ghost?" he managed to whisper. Truthfully, he couldn't imagine how. He had never heard of any ghost with such an . . . enticing body. She was very slender, yet her figure looked perfectly curved. Could a person be attracted to a ghost?

"Mm. Kind of. But kind of not."

The soft feminine voice had his eyes widening with shock. "You," he breathed. "You're my Etyrnal. You called to me."

"I did." She softly cupped his cheek with her hand and her eyes deepened as she smiled. "I want to protect you."

The smile turned a lovely face into an unforgettable one. The oddest déjà vu filled his mind and soul. He felt as if he had seen her somewhere before. His pulse began to beat a little harder, longing starting to eke through his exhaustion. "I've never been protected before."

"Yes, you have. You just never knew." She softly brushed her lips across his forehead and then got to her feet. "Can you stand and walk just a while longer? I want to take you and Kae somewhere safe until the healer I have sent for arrives."

"Your name?" He asked it as he got to his feet. His eyes followed her movements in fascination. The white clothing she wore was as wispy and haunting as the rest of her, and he was *sure* her feet didn't touch the ground. "Tell me your name."

"Gardina Campbell."

"Miss Campbell . . ."

"Gardina." The dimples appeared near her eyes again. "Or Ghosty. It's what my friends call me."

He wasn't shocked. "Gardina . . . why me? What is a Devotion?"

"That is best left for another time," she said softly. "Come with me, Matthias. You need food and rest. Kae needs a healer." She turned to walk into the woods but paused. "I am about to take you to my home," she admitted. "In all my Etyrnal life, only three others have ever visited my home. It sits just inside the border of Coronia. You will be safe there."

He got to his feet and lifted Kae in his arms. He could walk however much longer was needed. He was slightly amused at himself though. Crossing three countries within a matter of days. Then again, the Tri-Point was fairly good sized. With all the woods covering it, you could cross between countries a dozen times before figuring out your exact location.

With a sort of horrified fascination, he watched Gardina as they walked. Or rather, as he walked. She *floated*. He looked and looked again, and though her feet moved, he could swear she wasn't touching the ground.

Matt?

The soft stirring in his mind made his arms tighten around Kae. *What, little one?*

Ghosty is lonely like you.

He didn't respond to that. Instead, he asked Gardina, "Where can I find a healer for Kae?"

"I have sent for her already," she told him. She linked her hands behind her back. "Selene Lenroe is one of the most accomplished healers you'll ever meet.

She is a Dark Etyrnal, and she cherishes children the same as any Etyrnal."

"Does she have a Devotion?" he asked curiously.

A little smile teased her lips. "She used to. Things . . . changed. It may be another fifty years before she finds another."

He started to ask more questions when he realized they were walking into a small clearing in the woods. He stopped in his tracks, eyes wide as he stared at the disaster that passed for a building sitting not twenty feet away. Windows were boarded, holes pocked the walls, and the roof looked as if it would fall in at any moment. "You live there."

"Mm-hmm." Gold eyes twinkled merrily as she watched him.

"You *live* there."

"Well, 'live' is such a loose term," she murmured drolly. "I've never been certain if what I do is definable as 'living.' But it's not really 'death' either."

"You *live* there."

She burst into giggles and his gaze swung toward her swiftly. Mouth dry, he could only stare at her. He had never heard anything so . . . enchanting before. In her laughter, she looked innocent and carefree, as if the imp inside had never grown up. The hunger that had begun to prowl inside steadily grew.

Are you going to kiss her?

He hastily closed off as much of his mind to Kae as he possibly could. He cleared his throat. "I'm glad you find me amusing."

"Mortals amuse me," Gardina told him impishly. "Honestly, do you think that I'd keep the front in pristine condition if I wanted solitude? Don't worry. The inside is fully functional with all the latest amenities."

Reluctantly amused at both of them, he followed her to the front door and then inside. Lights from Runics came on immediately and he realized she had understated the case.

The house was, in fact, a manor. The foyer was grand and elegant with a set of curving staircases leading to a second floor. He could glimpse beyond the staircases what looked like a grand kitchen and dining room. Off to the right was a library and off to the left was what looked like a study.

The walls were covered with soft patterns of pale lavender and gold, and the floor was covered in cool tile. Anything that was made of wood was in a soft gray color. Just entering made him feel as if every burden on his shoulders had lifted.

"Follow me." She led the way upstairs, her heart beating a little harder. Knowing he liked her home brought her a sense of joy she hadn't expected. She wanted him to be happy. Safe. If she could have that, she would ask for nothing else.

She took him to one of the empty guest rooms and ushered him inside. "My cousin Vlad often stays here," she told him, "so he has left some clothes here. Feel free to bathe and change into something clean. Come downstairs when you're done and I'll make you something to eat." She held out her arms. "I'll take Kae."

He handed over his small cargo and found himself smiling as Gardina snuggled her close and buried her nose in Kae's fine brown hair. All Etyrnals cherished children, and no matter what else she might be, Gardina was no different in that.

She carried Kae to another room just down the hall and took her time getting the little girl more comfortable. She checked the wounds trying to heal naturally, removed all traces of dirt and sweat, and snuggled Kae into a warm blanket. It got cold in the woods at night.

Hearing water running in the bathroom down the hall, she let herself drift through the floor and down into the kitchen. Humming softly to herself, she got busy making food. Kae was sustaining herself on Matthias' lifeforce; as long as he kept healthy, she didn't need actual food.

Everything turned to silvery color around Gardina. She didn't look up from the vegetables she was cutting, even when she sensed her companion leaning on the counter across from her. "How much danger is he in?" She transferred the vegetables to a cooking pot.

The other woman tilted her head slightly. "More than you might expect." She handed over a jar of spice when Gardina reached for it. "Things have become . . . complicated."

"To say the least," she muttered. Her sharp ears detected the sound of footsteps and she sighed. "Why do things have to be complicated?"

"It's how you know you're alive, little ghost." And with that, she was gone.

The light returned to normal just as Matthias walked into the kitchen. He wore a pair of pants and a tunic, both plain but sturdy, and quite big on him despite his size. "Your cousin is huge," he informed her. He rolled up the sleeves and walked over to sit on one of the seats pulled up to the other side of the counter. His wet black hair clung to his face and neck and there was more color in his face now.

She checked the broth, found it ready, and poured some into a bowl for him. As he started to eat, she sat on the top of the counter to keep him company. "Feeling better?"

"Immensely. I think I washed off five layers of dirt. Please don't be offended if I fall asleep right after I eat."

"I won't be. You need rest." Her finger traced the faint pattern in the stone of her countertop. "I'm going to try to keep you safe, Matthias. I promise."

He pointedly stirred his broth without looking up. "Can I ask some personal questions?"

Her lips curved. "I'm three hundred years old. I was twenty when I found the Ghost Runic."

His head came up sharply. "You . . . you have a Greater Runic?" His gaze lowered to where the gray tribal mark was visible over the top of the laces of her bodice. He had assumed it was a clan marking of some kind since Runics were never fused to the heart. "I didn't think I'd ever meet an Etyrnal with one."

"I've never met another," she admitted. "All Greater Runics have been worn at some point in time since there are Etyrnals of all kinds running around, but that does not mean they are still worn."

"Including yours?"

She shook her head. "I am the only one of me. My Runic has never been worn by another."

"Why is it . . . there? Aren't Runics fused to the hand?"

Her gaze lowered. "That is . . . complicated. Can we discuss it later?"

Sensing the pain inside the request, he reluctantly shelved it. "So are you a Light or Dark Etyrnal?"

"Neither and both all at the same time." She gave a little shrug. "I'm called the Gray Etyrnal. Mine is the only Runic that is neither Light nor Dark but instead both. My Ghost Runic is named for the thirteenth moon called Ghost, which is gray. I do not lose my strength during the day or night, and instead I have access to different abilities depending on whether I am in the sun or moon."

He took a deep breath. "And Etyrnals really . . ."

"Drink blood? Yes." She found a smile. "It sustains the power of their immortal bodies. But they can, if they want, consume food as well. After all, their bodies *do* live. They just can't bear children and they are vulnerable in the day or night when their powers are weak."

"You say 'they.' What about you? I mean . . ." He got to his feet and put the bowl in the sink before stepping closer and leaning on the counter beside her. "You're an Etyrnal, but you're not Light or Dark. And you're not exactly *living*, I don't think."

She leaned closer and lightly rested her hand on his heart. "Me? Oh, sometimes." Her giggles burst out as he hastily scrambled back. "Your face!" She covered her mouth with her hands as her eyes danced merrily. "If you could see your face!"

He blew out a hard breath as he remembered that a mischievous, rather morbid, sense of humor was common among Etyrnals. "Very funny." Still, he smiled. He loved the sound of her laughter. "Seriously."

"Seriously," she said quieter, "I drink blood as well. The critical difference between I and my brethren is that there are restrictions on the blood I can consume. There needs to be an exceptionally high magical concentration in the blood of whomever I am feeding from. And . . . it has to be fresh. Not bottled."

Blood could be magically removed from a body and used to transfer to a wounded person or to feed an Etyrnal. There were, in fact, specialized hospitals that dealt with that only, offering a source for Etyrnals to obtain nourishment from when feeding from a living person was not possible. There were few people in the world who had never been bitten. But it was also true that there were few people who knew they had. Etyrnals took care to harm no one at all.

"How do you get by?" he asked her softly. He gently covered her hand with his.

"I have my ways. Don't worry. You won't suddenly wake and find me biting your neck or something. Actually, we rarely go for the neck unless we're, uhm, intimate with the person. We usually aim for the forearm."

"*Could* you use my blood?" When she hesitated, he caught her chin with his other hand and lifted it. "If that silence is a yes, then if you need me, tell me. I owe you, Gardina." He lowered his head to hers. "I owe you my life and my sanity. Your voice was my lifeline, and now you're saving me and Kae both. Giving you my blood is the least I can do."

"Thank you, Matt," she said softly, sincerely, "but I can't use your blood. You're my Devoted."

"Would you mind telling me now precisely

what a Devoted is?" he asked quietly. "Because I get the feeling I really ought to know."

She took a deep breath. "A Devoted is a person who was born under the full moon, but it gets more complicated than that. It has to be a full moon that is the *only* full moon. That happens much more rarely. If there is a Dark or Light Etyrnal who draws power from that moon, then if they meet a person born under their moon, they . . . bond. We call it a Devotion because that's what it comes down to. The Etyrnal is devoted to protecting their, uhm, charge."

He absorbed that for long moments. "So you've had other Devotions before?" It was an oddly unsettling and upsetting idea.

There was a soft pause before she admitted softly, "No. You are my first Devotion. The Ghost Moon is very, *very* rarely ever full by itself because it is Gray. In my three centuries, you are the first and only child born on the night of a full Ghost Moon." She made a light gesture. "You might be the last. I can't be sure."

"The gods rarely reveal their intentions," he said on a sigh. Something flickered across her face and his brows came together. "You don't believe in Light and Dark."

"I saw the afterlife." Her voice was very neutral. "And there was nothing there."

There was a hidden pain in her voice and he reached out without thought to softly cover her cheek with his hand. Her skin seemed almost ridiculously soft, and her bones were small underneath. She should have been a princess and not a Ghost Hunter. "I'm sorry," he told her softly. "To lose your belief must be hard."

"I've had time to get over it." She tried to lean away from his touch but he persisted. With a sigh, she gave in. Maybe the Devotion thing went two ways. Sure as hell Niall hadn't been in *his* right mind when he had met Selene.

"So . . ." He forced himself to remove his hand and step back. "Why would you feeding off me be bad? Or is it some sort of respect thing? Does it hurt and go against your determination to protect me?"

"To answer the last question, a bite doesn't hurt when it comes from an Etyrnal. For those of incompatible hormones, there's literally nothing to feel. Just a tiny little prick, like getting poked softly by a needle. For compatible hormones," her lips curved, "it can be much more enjoyable."

Jealousy swam inside him and he firmly shelved it. "You said for Etyrnals. Is there something else that bites?" A sudden chill roughened his skin. "Is . . ." He dropped his voice. "Is there really such a thing as a *nosferatu*?"

There was a silence, then, softly, "Do not ask questions for which you are not ready to hear the answers to."

"Then tell me why you can't bite me." His lips quirked up. "I think we both can tell we're *compatible*. Or is that part of the problem too?"

She waved her hand back and forth in the air. "Smaller problem, really. That kind of thing can be handled. No, it is because you are Etyrnal Sensitive. Being a Devoted, you hold a particular affinity for the moons. If a Devoted is bitten by their Etyrnal during every differing phase of their shared moon . . ."

His heart stopped. "I see. So that's how Etyrnals are made."

"Well, normal Etyrnals." She took a deep breath. "I am a True Etyrnal, possessing a Greater Runic. It is very, *very* possible that one single bite at any time our moon is in the sky could transform you."

"Alright. So, no biting. Got it." He hesitated and then asked softly, "Do most Devoted become Etyrnals eventually?"

It was her turn to hesitate. "I wouldn't say *most*. Many do. I won't lie about that. Many Etyrnals believe that Light and Dark place Devoted on the land to compensate for the fact that Etyrnals cannot procreate normally. It's hogwash. The moons affect everything on our world. It's just nature. All species need ways to procreate."

"I see." He took a step back. "I think that's enough questions for now. I am going to go sleep." He tilted his head slightly. "It is very late. Will your healer be here by morning?"

"No. She will arrive tomorrow night. If she arrived during the day, she'd be of no use because she'd have no power. I have no doubt you will sleep all tomorrow, but if you wake, feel free to explore the manor." She smiled. "There is no place you could go where you are not welcome."

"In that case, I will say good night. Good night, Ghosty."

"Good night, Matt." She watched him walk out and then let out the breath she had been holding. Compatible hormones. Well, that was one way of putting it.

Chapter Three

It was nearly evening when Matthias awoke from the deep sleep he had fallen into right after getting into bed. For the first time in months, he woke and felt refreshed. There was no rush to battle. There was no new list of casualties to look at. He had slept his share and then some.

He took another shower to help erase the lingering fogginess and then dressed in fresh clothes. Just showering and having clean clothes was an oddly novel feeling. And as he watched the sleeves go slightly past his hands, he was bemused anew. Just how big *was* Gardina's cousin?

The manor was quiet and still. Kae was asleep, her presence quiet inside his mind. He followed the connection to her room and found her sleeping contentedly with a stuffed toy in her arms. She was covered in fresh bandages, but the color in her face looked oddly good. Her thirst to live seemed unrivaled. She would indeed be a brilliant Runic Master one day.

Since he had been told he had free reign, he found himself wandering the halls and peeking into rooms. One room looked like it was used frequently, so he had to assume it was for the Dark Etyrnal that

Gardina had said was coming.

At the end of the hall, he found himself standing in front of a closed door that had been grayed by age. Since he had noticed the other doors had been refinished at times, he knew this had to be Gardina's room. For a moment, he hesitated and then he quietly opened the door to glance inside.

Whatever he had been expecting of Etyrnals fell short of the mark. A little smile tugged at his lips as he walked over to look at the bed where his hostess slept. He had half expected to see her looking, well, like the dead.

Instead, she was sleeping sprawled on her stomach over the majority of her small bed. One hand hung down the side. The other held a pillow over her head. The sheets and blankets tangled around her waist and legs, and the sleeveless sleeping gown she wore slipped down her shoulders.

The room was pitch black except for a tiny gray lamp giving enough light that Matthias could see. Both shutters and curtains blocked out the sunlight from even attempting to get in. He vaguely remembered hearing that Etyrnals couldn't sleep in light, whether sun or moon, so it made sense.

Gardina made a grumpy noise suddenly and

pulled the pillow off her head. She didn't entirely wake, however, and instead rolled over onto her side and burrowed under the covers. He quietly knelt beside her so he could study her face. She was absolutely flawless. Skin so pale should have appeared sickly, but it just added to her translucent, ethereal beauty.

Testing himself, he leaned in and softly touched her lips with his. She sighed softly, and a faint blush of pink came to her face. Tempted, beyond tempted, he wisely stood and left the room.

He went downstairs and made himself something to eat. As he was cleaning up after, he realized he could sense when the sun went down and Gardina awoke. It felt like a soft hum of power across the back of his mind. Odd how he hadn't noticed her presence inside him until it went away. It had to be another Devoted thing.

Quite suddenly, he felt a predatory presence and very slowly turned around to look at the entry. The other male standing in the doorway was not much shorter than his six-two height, lean like a hunter, and ruthlessly attractive. His hair was diamond white, his eyes pale blue, and his face was slightly angular in a way that indicated a Desertia heritage. In appearance, he looked no younger than

Matthias, but the little smirk in the corner of his eye indicated something more. Something . . . Etyrnal.

"So," the man said, the word clipped and drawled all at the same time, "you're the Bleeder that has caught our Ghosty's devotion." Derisive blue eyes ran over Matthias with slight mockery not at odds with the mockery in his accented voice. "Though why she'd bother with a Rikan soldier is beyond me."

Matthias crossed his arms. "It's nice to meet you too."

"Ha!" The Dark Etyrnal's eyes lit with genuine humor. "Nice to see some spunk in there. What's your name, fledglin'?"

"Matthias Logan." Matthias gave a slightly mocking salute.

It was countered by a slightly mocking bow. "Niall Lenroe. Never had my own last name. Decided to take my wife's." His white teeth flashed in his smile, revealing slightly sharpened incisors. "Selene went to take a look at the young patient of ours. Your daughter?"

"No. It's . . . complicated. She was wounded in war. Innocent blood. I couldn't just let her die. And . . . I was ready to leave. Gardina was my sanity. She told me to find her. So I did." Abruptly realizing how much he was saying, guardedness entered Matthias' eyes.

"No worries, fledglin'," Niall told him, "as I've been a Devoted myself not that long ago. I know how it feels." His teeth flashed in his smile again. "But I'm still older than you."

"Niall!"

The blond jumped nearly two feet in the air at the sound of Gardina's voice. "Now Ghosty," he started.

"Don't you 'now' me, fledgling!" Gardina shoved him out of the way. "Stop provoking Matthias." She stopped in front of Matthias and smiled up at him. "Ignore Niall. It's often safer. Selene is with Kae and says there won't be any problems with healing her back to good as new."

"That's one less worry," he said softly. A little smile quirked his lips. "It's going to be odd not having her so constantly in my head. I've gotten used to it."

"And there's such space in there," came a drawled retort.

"Niall!" Gardina narrowed her golden eyes on her friend.

With a distinct mutter, Niall turned and walked

out. Matthias wisely said nothing as he sat at the counter to watch Gardina assemble something for Kae to eat when she was healed. It was no hardship to watch Gardina. He was beginning to love the way she drifted across the ground. She was so utterly feminine that he was reminded of his own strength and masculinity. Getting intimately acquainted with their elemental differences was steadily growing more and more important.

"Compatible hormones," he muttered softly.

Proving she had ears like a cat, she said amiably, "They can be a pain in the ass. But we're old enough to find some self-control." A little twinkle was in her eye as she added, "At least until we know each other better."

He drank his coffee and looked for a different subject. "So how much older than me is Niall?"

"Hmm." She cocked her head slightly. "About ten years or so. He's been a Dark Etyrnal for five. He was Selene's Devoted. I've known Selene since the night I became an Etyrnal. Even then she was an Elder. I *think* she's close to a thousand years old. But even though she's older, I'm more powerful. She was a Devoted where I am a True Etyrnal."

"How old were you when you were changed? You look so young."

"That's actually an aberration," she explained dryly. "If a Devoted becomes an Etyrnal as a child, they will continue to grow and develop to their peak. At that point, they cease aging. If old when they become an Etyrnal, they will *reverse* age until they once more reach their peak. Being an Etyrnal is a preservation of the peak of a body. Sickness is removed. Youth is maintained or restored."

"What about you?" he persisted.

She let out a long sigh. "Matt, not now. You've had enough info thrown at you without going into the, erm, *gray* area around Runics and rebirth." She blinked as he came around the counter. "What?" She warily eased back as he eased in, his hands going to the counter on each side of her hips. "Matt . . ." she said warningly.

"I just want it known that I like our *compatible hormones*." He bent his head to skim his lips across the soft skin of her cheek. Her flesh warmed under his touch and he felt an answering throb of heat in his blood. He pressed a little closer and let her feel the heaviness of his hunger for her.

Her breath caught in her chest as his hands

shifted to her waist and pulled her flush against his hard body. It should have been impossible that one man produce that much heat, but he was wonderfully hot and strong. The heat seeped into even the coldest parts of her heart. An answering ache spread inside her, knotting inside her body until she quivered with need.

Their destination was inevitable. It was the getting there that felt a little frightening. The desire to protect him and ensure his happiness was not quite at odds with the additional desire for his body. And blood. That little seed was planted and growing. And growing. The ferocious urge to taste him had her incisors aching. "Matt."

The touch of fear in her voice had him lifting his head. He could see the swirl of gray inside her golden eyes that meant her power was on the rise. He ran a thumb across her lips and felt the sharpened point of a tooth. "I didn't mean to tease," he said softly.

"Then back up. Now." When he did, she let out a ragged breath. "I'm going hunting." With a swirl of light and dark entwined, she disappeared from right in front of him.

Niall cleared his throat and Matthias turned to look at him. There was a moment of silence, then Niall said sympathetically, "I would say it will get better, fledglin', but I'm afraid it will only get worse."

Matthias just sighed. "Yeah. I figured you'd say that."

Upstairs, Selene Lenroe had discovered that her young patient was really an imp changeling. The healthier Kae became, the more she got restless and fidgety. She was *tiny*, though, and that very smallness had Selene sincerely questioning her origins. There was a lot of power packed in Kae's body, and it was such an odd amalgam that Selene had never seen the like before.

As soon as the wounds were fully sealed, she needed to test the blood level of Kae's body to make sure she wasn't too badly deficient. For an Etyrnal, the easiest way to test blood level was to consume it. Not wanting to frighten Kae, she scooped the little girl onto her lap. "Give me your hand."

Kae solemnly held up her hand. She trusted this lady. She was really pretty with her dark chocolate skin and pale cream-colored eyes! The touch of her power felt like darkness. It was warm and comforting, and fiercely protective. "If you bite me, will I be like you?"

"No." Selene smiled. "You'd have to be born on the full moon of the

Millennium Moon for that. If you're a Devoted, you are not mine. Don't worry. This won't hurt."

In fascination, Kae watched as Selene very gently bit her finger. Really, it didn't hurt at all. Etyrnals were kind of strange but really kind of interesting too. Was Ghosty an Etyrnal? Did she drink blood? She bit back as many questions as she could.

Speculation filled Selene's eyes as she regarded Kae. The child was not entirely Human. However much Fae blood there was in addition to her Human blood, it was hard to say, but she was definitely *not* just Human. "Well, your blood level is a little low, but nothing some good food and rest won't fix. Matthias did a fine job of protecting you."

Kae nodded solemnly. "He's gonna adopt me. But he doesn't know yet."

A smile tugged at Selene's lips. Matthias, and by proxy Gardina, were both doomed. "Your secret is safe with me, little one. Now let's go meet him properly, shall we?"

Downstairs, Gardina had returned from her hunt. Clearly more on level ground, she was comfortable once more with Matthias. It was to his fascination, however, that he noticed she was glowing ever so softly. There were times where she was truly more ghost than flesh and blood.

When Selene stepped into the doorway, his jaw dropped. It promptly sent Niall and Gardina into a fit of laughter. He barely heard them. He had *never* seen such a regal woman before. She was flawlessly beautiful and carried such an aura of power that it seemed to pulse in the air.

"Oh hush!" Selene told her husband crossly as she walked over to him. She firmly pinched his ear between two fingers. "As I recall, you had much the same reaction! Except you fell on the ground."

"And that's why we're amused." He snagged her hand and brought it to his lips for a moment. "Y'have such a wonderful effect on people of all types."

Gardina giggled softly. "I don't recall reacting like this when *I* met you the first time, but there were other factors going on at the time."

Selene contemplated the confused and volatile state she had found her young friend in right after obtaining her Runic. "That is one way of putting it." She smiled at Matthias. "Hello, I am Selene Lenroe."

Bemused, he smiled back. What the hell had happened to his life? "Matthias Logan." His gaze lowered and he saw a pair of pale green eyes peeking at him around Selene's leg. They were set into a familiar, delicate face. His smile spread. "Kae?"

"Matt!" With a happy cry, the little girl dashed across the kitchen and leapt up into his arms with far more agility than her age and size gave credence to. It was almost as if she flew.

"Hey there." He hugged her as tightly as he dared and buried his face in her red curls. "How do you feel?"

"Lots better." She nodded solemnly. She was very careful to hide her thoughts since they seemed to be maintaining their mental link. She didn't want to scare him off, and he might scare if he knew he was the perfect daddy and she was determined he be hers. He just smelled . . . right. "Selene says that I'm as good as new."

"Thank you," he told Selene. "I know it isn't needed but . . . thank you."

"Of course." She sat down beside Niall with a smile. "Etyrnals cherish children; even if she hadn't belonged to you and therefore to Ghosty, I would have needed to help."

As if remembering, Kae immediately focused on Gardina. She had never actually *seen* her before, and when she saw her now, she found herself completely unsurprised. Gardina looked exactly like Kae had expected her to, yet somehow even prettier and softer. "Are you really a ghost?" she demanded. "Can you go through walls?"

"Not entirely," Gardina said dryly, "and yes."

Kae assessed what she felt, had heard, and understood, then stated, "Matt wants to kiss you."

Niall coughed. Selene pretended an interest in her nails. Matthias felt his cheeks heating slightly. He wasn't the only one. Gardina knew a blush was climbing her neck as well. "Yes," she finally said. "I know."

"Are you going to let him?"

"You ask too many questions," she scolded lightly. "When I was your age, my father and mother would tie gags on me and my sister if we talked too much."

Kae's eyes went wide. "Oh." She *really* wanted to ask how old Gardina was, but she didn't want to make her mad *or* get herself gagged. "Breakfast?" she asked hopefully instead.

"That we can do." Matthias put her down on a chair and then picked her up again when her head barely reached the top of the table. "Well, that won't work."

"Hold on." Niall left the kitchen only to come back with several thick books. He put them on the chair. "Let's try this."

Matthias put Kae on the books and they lifted her to the right height to reach the table. Gardina put a plate of food in front of her, and blessed silence fell as Kae happily started eating. She was *starving*.

Matthias watched her with a little smile. He had never really been around children much, though he wasn't been overly wary of them either, as some soldiers could be. From the get-go, however, he had felt perfectly comfortable with Kae. Whatever he decided to do with his life, if he could keep Kae as his daughter, he would happily do it. He hadn't expected to love her so much or so easily.

The smile teasing his lips was more tempting to Gardina than she liked. She really, *really* wanted to kiss him. She wanted to get her hands into his hair and feel his hands on her body. She could even feel her incisors throbbing lightly, indicative that she wanted more than even that.

On a low sound of frustration, she walked out of the kitchen. She had no doubt that she and Matthias would be lovers. They would go mad if they weren't. The seed of fear had planted in her heart, though.

Could she control herself enough to keep from biting him while they made love? The Ghost Moon was in the sky most of the time during this part of the year. Only on occasional days was it hidden.

She went into her office and sat down at her desk. With a groan, she dropped her head on her arms. "This bites." As she heard her own words, she rapped her head on the desk. "Damn it, I'm not helping things by making Etyrnal puns."

"Compatible hormones," Selene said gravely from the doorway. "Always worse when a Devoted is involved."

"You'd know!" Gardina lifted her head with a scowl. "Why didn't you warn me that this would happen? I'm thinking that if it has happened twice, it happens more."

"It happens quite frequently," Selene admitted. She walked into the office and sat on the edge of the desk. "Not every time, of course. Of the Devoted I have known, two were of compatible hormones. Another was Niall. The other three were like my children. I have every expectation that any other Devoted that I, or Niall, have will be of that similar ilk. Such is the way of our life. Our Mother and Father plan for all."

Gardina ignored that. "A warning would still have been nice."

"I might have warned you if I had realized you'd have a Devoted," Selene said bluntly. "In the last several centuries, only *once* has the Ghost Moon been full by itself. That was the night that Matthias was born. No other children were born that night. It is a bit surprising that he was born then, I might add, because the Ghost Moon is known to negate the powers of Life and Death equally."

"A night of suspension," Gardina murmured. "None die. None born. How appropriate." She straightened and ran her hands through her hair. "I'm not really worried about being his lover, you know. He wouldn't be my first. He is a good man, and I care very deeply for him. But I am a True Etyrnal."

"And that certainly does run risky this time of year." Selene cocked her head. "What if you fall in love with him, Ghosty? What if he falls in love with you?"

Her hands clenched together. "We'll cross that bridge if we get to it."

"Do you think you might?"

Her friend smiled sadly. "I think it might be too late. I don't know, though. I've never been in love before. How did you know you were in love with Niall?"

"Hmm." Selene frowned as thought about it. "I couldn't say it was any one sign for me. For either of us. We had something so . . . *profound* between us. Emotionally and physically. I'd never responded to anyone as I had to him, not even my other Devoted. And he was certainly in over his head too! Everything finally added up."

Gardina didn't have other Devoted to compare to, but she could at least be sure that what she and Matthias might have definitely fell under the 'profound' heading. She would have to take it a step at a time and figure out where things went. She was not opposed to transforming him should that be what *he* wanted, whether to have a permanent relationship with her or simply because he would rather be an Etyrnal. "Hearts make life so complicated."

Selene smiled. "But much more enjoyable."

The study door banged open as Niall rushed inside. Fury lit his blue eyes. "We have a problem, ladies." His accent came out more clipped than drawled as evidence of his temper. "There's a Bleeder approachin'."

The use of the term 'Bleeder' for non-Etyrnals was one of the most offensive derogatory names out there. "Is he not turning back from the appearance?" Selene asked.

"He's wearing a Rikan soldier uniform."

Gardina shot to her feet. "What sort of uniform?"

"He's a hunter."

She said something uncomplimentary under her breath. There were three types of hunters in the world. Her kind, which hunted because of a need, another kind who hunted those with prices on their heads, and a third that hunted who or whatever they were told as long as they were paid enough. There would be no reason for either of the first type to approach. It had to be the third—and he was after Matthias.

She pushed past Niall and went into the kitchen. Matthias and Kae were still at the table though they were done with their food. Both wore similar pensive expressions. "You need to hide," Gardina told them briskly. "And don't argue with me. I'm nice, but I'm not a pushover."

Matthias said nothing as he picked up Kae and followed Gardina out of the kitchen. She took them to the foyer and then lightly touched her Runic mark.

Gray power swirled around her body and down to the ground. An invisible trapdoor appeared and she opened it. Matthias climbed down the ladder without protest. It went against the grain to let her handle alone whatever problem was approaching, but he knew not to test her stubbornness. "Gardina?"

She shook her head. "There's no time." She followed them inside and shut the trapdoor overhead. She sealed it with power once more and then turned translucent. "This bunker can withstand *anything*. It can only be opened by me, and it is reinforced by my Runic. Not even another Greater Runic could penetrate the Ghost Runic's defenses." She reached out and tenderly brushed her fingers down Matthias' cheek though he could not feel the touch. "You are my Devoted. I cannot let you be harmed. I respect your strength, Matt. Never doubt that."

He had never wanted to hold anyone more than he wanted to hold her in that moment. "Be careful."

"I can't die." She drifted up through the ceiling without anything more.

His gut twisted. She might not be able to die, but that didn't mean she couldn't be hurt. Couldn't bleed and cry. There were many fates worse than death, unfortunately.

Selene and Niall, being Dark Etyrnals, were at their greatest power during the night. They met up with Gardina as she left the manor and stood on the steps to confront the figure approaching. The Ghost Hunter's sharp eyes evaluated her intruder. He looked relatively young, though an adult, and he had a crossbow in his hand. He had an interesting wavery effect to his aura; mortals very rarely had such a thing unless they were of exceptional power. Kae's aura wavered, too.

Gardina frowned. There was something odd about this mortal. She could not put her finger on it, but it was there. She gave him points for nerve, though; not even Etyrnals dared approach her manor without invitation. It had stood for over three centuries in the same spot, and it was considered a landmark of Coronia. The queen before last had even decreed it a protected space, which meant instant dungeon time if you damaged it. Considering the condition Gardina let it appear outside, few bothered approaching at all.

This hunter from Rikan either did not know the law or did not care. She was inclined to suspect the latter. "Halt and state your business," she ordered.

He stopped but he said nothing. He merely tugged aside his cloak to reveal the quiver on his hip. It was filled with silver-tipped arrows. Selene and Niall immediately faded into the darkness of the woods, and both were cursing. Silver, being of the Light, could do lethal damage to a Dark Etyrnal. Likewise, gold, being of the Dark, could do the same to Light Etyrnals.

Gardina, being Gray, feared neither silver nor gold. In the same way neither the sun nor the moon could weaken her, she could repel the effects of both metals. She merely lifted a brow and noted coolly, "You do not belong here."

"Stand aside, Etyrnal, or I'll put an arrow in you first," he retorted.

"How cute. I am the Gray Etyrnal, mortal. I am True. Your arrows are worthless against me, providing you could even hit me." Her body went translucent and back again as proof. "Get off my property."

"You're the Ghost Hunter I heard about." Satisfaction filled his voice. "And if you are the Gray Etyrnal, then my target is here. Hand him and the child over."

That was interesting. Rikan wanted Kae as

well? Perhaps there truly was something special about her. "Ha. Funny." Her eyes narrowed warningly. "Matthias Logan is my Devoted. I will hand him over to *no one.*" Power moved over her body warningly. "I will not let you even breathe the same air as him."

"And how will you stop me?" He held up a fire Runic and smirked when she visibly paled. The specter form that ghosts had, and she could take, was effectively a mist. It could be burned by a hot enough fire, and if exposed for too long, they evaporated entirely. It was sketchy if Gardina could actually be killed, but she would assuredly be damaged viciously.

She could not risk the chance that she got hurt too badly to protect Matthias. Her stomach clenched with the understanding of the sacrifice she needed to make but there was *nothing* more important than her Devoted's safety. She went translucent and disappeared back into the manor. She drifted down through the invisible trapdoor to the hidden basement, but she misjudged her height before going corporeal. She landed with a thump on the ground. "Owie!"

"Gardina!" Matthias knelt beside her and swiftly ran his hands over her. "Are you okay? Did you hurt yourself?" A distant part of him had to be amused at himself despite the situation. He had seen some incredibly gruesome injuries and yet a simple fall had panicked him.

"I'm fine," she hastily assured him and then stifled a surprised squeak when his hands skimmed over her breasts. "Matt!"

"What?" He saw where his hands had landed and quickly pulled them away. He hadn't intended to get *quite* that personal. Not yet anyway. "Er, sorry."

She huffed out a little breath and moved over to where Kae was sitting against a wall. He watched her move and then looked down at his hands. He could still feel the heat and softness of her flesh. Compatible hormones. Such a blasé, unassuming, phrase for something so potentially explosive. He had a feeling he might be closer to obsession and craving than anything else. If he didn't kiss her soon, didn't get to watch her eyes melt and her skin flush, he would go mad.

"I'm hot," Kae complained.

He hastily checked himself, but she had finally lost her direct route to his conscious thoughts. As soon as he realized that, he also realized what she was feeling. The bunker was getting exceptionally warm. It took longer for him to notice the change thanks to his time in the desert, but as soon as he did notice, he was uncomfortable. "What's going on?" He climbed the ladder and touched the invisible door. It was far warmer than it should be for being underground.

He glanced at Gardina and the absolute misery in her eyes clued him in. Her home was on fire. He had felt from the beginning that her manor was her sanctuary, and the agony in her darkened gold eyes seemed to prove it. "Why didn't you fight?" he whispered.

"Not even ghosts—or ghostys—can escape fire." Her hands clenched together. "I couldn't risk being too badly injured that I couldn't protect you. Matt . . . there was a hunter here looking for you and Kae. He knew about Selene and Niall, and he knew you were my Devoted. I don't know how he knew, but I do know this: someone was watching you at your camp. You were under surveillance the entire time."

His mouth opened and closed. "But I never once gave any sign I would leave!" he protested. "I didn't even know I *could* leave until you suggested it! I wouldn't have done it if it hadn't been for Kae!" He grabbed her arms. "You shouldn't have sacrificed your safety for mine!"

"You are my Devoted," she said again, quieter. "You are everything in this world that I must protect."

Though she did not use the small "L" word that encompassed it all, he could still hear it. He could not say what sort of love she felt. He could not even say what sort of love *he* felt, though he knew it was there. Only time would reveal that. He would be damned if he let anyone cheat them out of the time they needed to determine what they had.

Kae looked at the misery on Gardina's face and saw the tears shimmering across her eyes. Fury began to beat inside her heart that anyone would hurt her Ghosty. "Matt, make it stop! Ghosty needs her home!"

"I can't," he said helplessly. "I would if I could."

"I want it to stop!" Her voice rose with every word until the last word was shouted. Her voice echoed in the tiny cellar and it was echoed by an eerily loud roll of thunder from far, far overhead. The thunder was followed by the sound of a storm breaking open and rain pounding against the ceiling. The heat evaporated into a chill.

Matthias and Gardina looked at the ceiling only to sense a glow behind them. They both turned and found Kae on her knees. She started crying as she clasped her hands around her head in pain. The glow rippled over her body and then finally dissipated. She nearly slumped over face first into the dirt but Matthias hastily caught her. She was unconscious before he lifted her. "Gardina?"

"I genuinely don't have a clue." She looked up as the rain stopped pounding and sounded more like a very light rain. She unsealed the trapdoor and climbed the ladder to open it. She exited the bunker, and Matthias followed her.

Very little remained of the manor. Even if the rain hadn't come when it had, there wouldn't have been much left to burn. The air was filled with smoke and mist, and it smelled of burnt wood and greenery. Matthias felt sick to his stomach as he remembered the aged gray door that had stood as the entrance to a three-century long sanctuary.

He looked to where Gardina was moving silently through the wreckage, and she was in her specter form. She seemed to have merged to the mist and yet he could see the tears running down her cheeks. His rage stirred. Someone would *pay* for breaking her heart. He was her Devoted? Well, that devotion went both ways. "I'll kill that bastard for this," he vowed softly.

"Stand in line, fledgin'," Niall said icily from behind him. "Stand in line."

Chapter Four

Matthias turned around and found Selene and Niall had rejoined them. The dark fury on Niall's face was oddly less alarming than the similar expression on his wife's face. Perhaps because Selene was older, more powerful, and far more even-tempered. Curiously, Matthias felt no fear of them. He never really had. Maybe it had to do with being a Devoted; after all, he possessed the potential to be an Etyrnal himself.

It was something still at the back of his mind. It did not actually bother him that he might be one someday. Etyrnals were really no different from Humans or Fae other than the fact that they drank blood. Fae had an unusual diet, too, or so he had heard. All races had their strengths and weakness, though the stronger the strength, the stronger the weakness.

If he was destined to be an Etyrnal—be it Light, Dark, or Gray—he would accept it willingly. After all, being an Etyrnal would give him *plenty* of time to evaluate just how compatible his and Gardina's hormones were together. It was a tempting thought, and understanding that told him his feelings were probably deeper than he thought.

The gut-wrenching pain he felt as he watched Gardina drift among the ruins was another clue. "How long did she live here?" he asked Niall in a low voice.

Niall tucked his hands in his pockets. Empathy darkened his eyes as he watched Gardina. "For as long as she has been an Etyrnal. It used t'be a royal manor of the Coronia Kingdom, but they turned it over to her. Not long ago, they named it a landmark to keep it safe—for her, I've always thought. I've never asked why the kingdom cared. I reckoned it was none of my business."

It was probably none of Matthias' business either, but he would still ask. Because only Niall would know, he asked softer, "Is how I feel normal?"

A hint of a smile softened the Etyrnal's face. "Reckon so, if you feel the way I did for Selene. It's a bloody pain trying to support and protect somethin' that could turn you into snack food, but it can't be stopped. Even platonic Devotions can be pretty damned powerful. Definitely goes both ways. It's just trickier when the *compatible* type promises to last forever."

It made Matthias feel better to know. He let out a quiet breath and turned his attention to something else. He offered Kae to Selene. "She got a headache during the storm and started glowing brightly. Even Gardina didn't know why."

Selene snuggled Kae close and gently healed away the lingering headache she could feel pounding in the girl's small head. "She is not wholly Human," she admitted. "I sensed it before. I don't know how much Fae blood she has, but she has some. Fae do have some natural elemental power related to the moons; it's why they can't equip Runics of any kind."

His brows shot up. "I didn't know that."

"It's a trade-off, basically." Selene probed through Kae's body with her power to see if she could pinpoint how much Fae power she possessed, but she encountered something else entirely. It shocked her enough that her eyes widened for a moment before narrowing. It was an unexpected development, to be sure.

"Selene?" Niall cocked a brow.

"She's roughly half-Fae. Can't be more than that. Might be less. The storm was assuredly hers, though." Her eyes met his for a moment with a promise to explain later. She smiled at Matthias instead. "She will be just fine."

Matthias took the fact that Kae was half-Fae in stride even though that made her *exceptionally* rare.

Fae and Humans were not that successful at crossbreeding. Of a thousand couples, *maybe* one might have a child. It was entirely possible that Kae was the only half-Fae alive in the world at all. "I can handle that." He smiled crookedly. "I'm the Devoted to the Gray Etyrnal. If I can handle that, I can handle a half-Fae."

Kae had begun to stir, and when she woke, Selene gently put her down. The small Fae immediately began to pick her way across the charred landscape to where Gardina was digging in the ashes. Selene considered her words and then said, "She is special. I don't think Kae even knows how special she is. She has natural abilities that are being enhanced."

"I had felt when I met her that she could be a Runic Master," Matthias admitted.

Runic Masters were a rare breed unto themselves. They were people who had the ability to equip and master any Runic they laid hands on. On top of that, they were exceptionally gifted with strong magic, and any Runic they wore would be of twice its normal strength. A normal fire Runic could start a blaze; a fire Runic with a Runic Master could instantly start an inferno. "She has the potential, to be sure," Selene agreed.

Niall had been listening, but he had also been watching Gardina. "What do we do now?"

Matthias studied him and Selene alike. "Why didn't you fight?"

The lack of condemnation in his voice kept Niall from rounding on him in anger. He already felt like shit. "We wanted to. The Bleeder had silver arrows. If he had hit one of us, we'd've been out for the count—if not dead. Silver is dangerous to Dark Etyrnals. Gold to Light ones, so y'know."

That explained that. Matthias had wondered why silver arrows were such a bad thing. "She sacrificed her home for me."

"Yeah, she did." Niall shrugged. "Get used to it. Selene did some damned stupid things for my hide—stuff I still haven't forgiven her for."

Selene didn't bother to tell him that she regretted nothing, and neither would Gardina. She knew that if their roles were reversed, she would feel the same way. "Matthias," she said gently, "do not waste time with guilt. Cherish being the Devoted of the Gray Etyrnal. I do not think anyone on this world loves as hard, long, and deep as she does. Until your dying day, she will always be right beside you. And if you are both blessed to be *in* love with each other, then your eternity will be far sweeter than even mine and Niall's."

"How will I know?"

"You just will." She gave him a little nudge. "Go to her." She watched him walk away and leaned her head against Niall's shoulder as he tugged her close. Truthfully? She already knew the answer. She just thought it would be much more wonderful for them to discover it for themselves.

Matthias walked slowly toward Gardina, and his gut twisted anew as he saw that there were tracks of tears through the soot on her face. Despite her jokes to the contrary, he knew she was far, far more alive than her Ghost Runic strictly implied. He knelt and reached out to grasp her hands. She tried to evade him but he persisted. Her fingers went limp in his grip and his eyes narrowed. "No shifting."

She reluctantly stopped changing form and went very still as his free hand began to wipe the soot from her face. She needed to be strong for him, but she wanted nothing more than to crawl into his arms and be protected for once. His gentleness destroyed her defenses. Try as she might, more tears welled and she tried to shake them off.

"You can cry," Kae told her as she moved closer. "It's okay to cry. You said so."

"I'm feeling better," Gardina lied without guilt. "Go play with Selene and Niall. I need to talk to Matt." She watched her scamper off and then turned back to her Devoted. "I don't want your guilt, Matthias. Or pity."

"I can't help feeling the first, but I don't feel the second at all. I hurt for you, Gardina, but I don't pity you. Pity is for those who are weak. You are an incredibly strong woman inside and out. I respect you, and I hurt that you were put into the position where you had to choose my safety over your own."

She let out a long breath. "Things happen. We can discuss later what all this may entail. As you said, you were loyal. There was no reason to doubt you." She freed a hand and briefly cupped his cheek. "I'll be okay. I have plenty of time to rebuild my home someday." She hesitated before easing up to barely brush her lips against his. "I would rather have been here to protect you than to have you alone," she said softly. "Let go of the guilt, Matt."

If it hadn't been for the two other Etyrnals and Kae, he would have pulled her closer for the kiss they both wanted. He instead released her entirely and got to his feet to walk back over to the others. Kae was clinging onto Niall's shoulders and asking a million questions. The fact that Niall took it in stride made Matthias re-evaluate him. Maybe he wasn't that much of an ass after all.

"I think this is yours," Niall told him dryly. He scooped up Kae and plopped her into Matthias' arms. "I reckon your guardian can answer your questions, little mite." He shot a smirk at Matthias. "He's smarter than I'd expect from a Rikan soldier."

Matthias muttered something uncomplimentary under his breath. Kae wrapped her arms around his neck and looked at him with wide eyes. "Is Ghosty okay? Can we rebuild her house? Are you my daddy now? Niall says you should be. Can Ghosty be my mommy? You watch her a lot. She makes you happy."

He sighed and covered her mouth with a hand. He wasn't entirely sure how to answer any of those questions other than the first. "Gardina will be fine." He looked over and found that the woman in question was approaching with a book in her hands. "Was that what you were looking for?" he asked curiously. He passed Kae back to Niall and then walked closer to

Gardina. The book looked like a thick journal. "I'm surprised it survived."

"Is that your log?" Selene asked.

"Yes to both." Gardina opened the book and thumbed through the pages. "It's a bit singed but otherwise intact." For Matthias' benefit, she explained, "When it is said that I am a Ghost Hunter, it is not merely because I am a ghost who hunts. I hunt ghosts. One of the strongest powers within my Runic is the ability to banish lingering spirits. The other is call back spirits that should not leave."

His eyes widened slightly. "You can cheat death."

She made a vague gesture. "It's not cheating when it is a natural gift. I can see the length of a life. If it is ending too soon, I bring it back. Kae was that way. If you had not interfered, I would have."

Everything happening was beginning to strongly sound and feel like destiny, but he kept that thought to himself. He did not begrudge her lack of belief; in fact, all he felt was pain. He wanted to find a way to make her believe again. "Okay, I can understand that. Why is the book important?"

"I keep track of people who are reported dead

but their ghosts are unaccounted for anywhere." She thumbed through pages.

"So they aren't dead?" He couldn't stomach the idea of looking at the list of names; it was far too much like the list of names he had been forced to read every day. Endless casualties of a useless war for a greedy bastard.

As if she had read his mind, she pointedly turned the book where he could not see it. "Some yes and some no. Some are probably alive, but others are just missing. Some spirits go into hiding once they are separate of their flesh. It happens especially with sudden death. These ghosts are the ones I hunt since they tend to be the ones that are the most dangerous. They can and will attack anything that crosses their path. Or they'll possess someone in order to get a body back."

Niall looked over her shoulder. "Well, there's confirmation of at least one 'not dead.' Your name is in here, Matthias."

"Of course it is." Gardina skimmed more pages. "My log is a magical artifact. It updates itself. I've always assumed it was made of Runics."

Under his breath, Niall muttered, "I still don't think any Runic could do that kind of thing. Smacks of godlike."

"Yeah, if there were gods maybe." She found the page she wanted. "Okay! Here are the names who disappeared on the same day as you, Matt. We have to assume that if they were watching you, then someone must have surely left right after you to follow you here. I'd bet he faked his death, too, in order to have the maximum freedom to do whatever he wanted."

Matthias looked at the page and recognized several names, but only one jumped out at him. "Darren Richards. Huh. He was my commanding officer."

Selene cocked a brow. "That puts him right between you and the king in hierarchy, doesn't it? I thought *you* were the commanding officer on the field."

"I was." He shrugged. "The king refused to promote a commoner to that high a position, so Richards had to hold it. It was mostly in name; I still gave the orders on the field. He would occasionally tell me what to do just to remind me he was higher ranked, but my soldiers ignored him. I couldn't say why he hated me—I just know he does. Also? He's a cold-blooded bastard."

Niall saw Kae's eyes widen and snorted softly. "Well, there goes her vocabulary."

"I don't care if she hears them as long as she refrains from saying them until she's an adult." Matthias frowned. "I still can't make sense of any of this. I can't imagine why they would assume I might turn traitor. I don't think I would have left if Kae hadn't arrived and Gardina hadn't already planted the idea in my head. Maybe Richards figured I'd grow to resent my lack of promotion."

"There's something missing in this picture," Gardina grumbled. She scowled. "If that was Richards who came knocking, then he knows more than he really should. He knew about me, knew about Selene and Niall, *and* he expressed interest in Kae—which given her gifts isn't a surprise. But how did they know about them at all?"

"Her ability to survive," Selena murmured. She looked to where the little girl was almost asleep with her head on Niall's shoulder. "No Human child could have survived what she did. Anyone who knows anything about the races would have pegged her as being partial Fae—and that makes her exceptionally rare and powerful."

"The only thing we can know for sure," Niall

said curtly, "is that y'all can't be staying here. He'll come back. I'm thinking it would be best if you made your way to Coronia Castle and asked for sanctuary."

"That's ages from here!" Matthias protested. "I can't take Kae on a journey that far!"

Selena shook her head. "We will care for her, Matthias. She will be very safe with us. You can get sanctuary and then we will bring Kae to you. The other option is to head for sanctuary and make your trip, hmm, obvious."

Gardina pursed her lips. "To lure out Richards where we can remove him. I like that."

He eyed her. "You're going to go with me?"

"Uhm, yes? What part of 'you're my Devoted' did you miss? Or the part where that jerk destroyed my house? Or the part where I kinda take offense at people threatening innocent kids? Or maybe even the part where I have an in with the kingdom and they're more likely to listen to me than you?"

The rational part of his brain said that she was more than capable of protecting herself and it was unlikely that *any* creature on the world could harm her. The not-so-rational part of his brain that was tangled up in a potent blend of potentially immortal emotions didn't want her anywhere near this mess when she had already suffered. Yet, in the end, it was those very emotions that made him give in. How could he figure out how he felt if she was not there? "Alright." He couldn't stop himself from brushing her hair out of her eyes. "Thank you."

With half of the night still remaining, they moved away from the wreckage into the deeper woods and set up a makeshift campsite. Kae was already asleep before Matthias tucked her into Niall's offered cloak. He reluctantly laid down for sleep as well. It was ridiculous for him to stay awake as a guard when the two Dark Etyrnals were most at home in the night. They were nocturnal; they wouldn't even be sleepy until the dawn.

The pros and cons of the three types of Etyrnal turned inside his mind as he watched the Ghost Moon in the sky. It was waning and would leave the sky within two weeks. It would not come back to the sky again for another year. Two weeks would be a long time to test his self-control, and Gardina's as well. The steadily increasing volatile state of their relationship promised to detonate sooner rather than later. Then again, as long as the Ghost Moon was hidden, they would be safe. Maybe he ought to try doing one of those rain dances the Fae had invented. Storm cover would hide the moon. Bemused at his own thoughts, he finally fell asleep.

Dawn was still an hour away when Gardina left the camp and headed back to the ruins of her home. The piles of ash and charred wood were even more depressing in the dimly lit night. No night was ever truly dark on the world. She had always assumed it was the balance of things. Light in the dark in the same way the sun brought shadows during the day.

The light around her turned to silver. Her ethereal companion stepped up beside her and murmured, "Even Etyrnals who live forever will form attachments to physical possessions. I am sorry, little ghost."

"It feels a bit like losing my family again," she admitted. "They gave me the manor because they knew I would never fit in any society. I don't belong to the dead and yet I don't belong to the living. Some adults don't even see me. Only the children see me consistently."

"Of course they do." The silver-haired Etyrnal held up a hand and a small white butterfly formed at her fingertips. The darkness beyond seemed to move forward and caress her legs with the intimacy of a lover. "Children are blessed to see both light and dark when they are young. As innocence fades, they choose their path to the moon or the sun. You are the symbol of their innocence. One could even say you are the innocence lost to adults."

"I am not wholly sure that's a compliment."

She smiled. "There is a longing for innocence inside Matthias. He has never known any. His childhood was stolen. His life has been only war. A Devoted always needs something only his or her Etyrnal can give. And in turn, a Devoted always gives something back that only he or she can. You are the innocence he needs."

"Then what does he give me?"

"You will figure it out soon enough." With a soft shimmer of light, she disappeared.

The light went back to normal as Gardina frowned at where she had stood. Not that she doubted Matthias had something to give to her, but she couldn't put her finger on what it might be. She would have been willing to argue *he* should have been the one to bring innocence to their relationship, but her sense of eternal optimism wholly contrasted his more grounded view. Strange how that worked when he believed in non-existent gods and she didn't.

She lightly touched her Runic mark and drew forth a small flute. Runics could carry very small objects within their magical depths as long as they were non-organic. She kept matches, her flute, and her logbook there. She lifted the flute to her lips and began to softly play, calling to the night birds to sing along and replace devastation with beauty.

Matthias stood at the edge of the trees and felt his throat close at the haunting melody. It seeped deep into his heart and dug in where it could never be removed. Somehow his burdens felt lighter. And yet, again, he could hear the painful loneliness inside her music. He slowly walked forward as if afraid she might disappear into the shadows.

She lowered the flute and turned to look at him. She said nothing. An odd fragility under the surface made him ache to hold her and take away her burdens. Somehow he was sure that he was the only one who could remind her that she was alive. He reached out and cupped her cheek. Her skin was cool yet warmed instantly. He had a dozen questions for her, but they were no longer important in that moment.

Her gold eyes lifted and met his green ones. *Do*

you know what I am? Her voice whispered softly through his mind.

It doesn't matter, he countered. *I want you exactly as you are. I would change nothing about you.*

She hesitated for a moment before drifting up off her feet to bring them eye-level. Her arms slowly slid around his neck. He drew her slowly closer until their lips finally touched. They were softer than he had imagined, and they also warmed quickly. He teased the corner with his tongue, and she promptly smiled. The impish curve was more than he could resist. He caught her close and kissed her the way he had wanted since the moment her soft voice had saved his sanity.

As tender as the kiss was, it made greedy stabs of desire clench inside her body. Hunger for his blood stirred along with hunger for his taste, and her incisors lengthened against her will. He barely paused as he discovered them. He just teasingly touched one with his tongue and kept on kissing her as if he had no intention of ever stopping.

The area grew dimmer as clouds came in to cover the night sky. The Ghost and Water Moons were hidden entirely, and only the Sovereign Moon managed to shed some red light to the land. Matthias framed Gardina's face in his hands and eased back enough to ask huskily, "Do you need me?"

She didn't pretend to misunderstand. "Yes." The pulse in his neck tempted and lured. She had only ever bitten anyone's wrist before, but his neck looked *really* bitable. His pulse all but had a 'place teeth here' sign. Before the fickle weather made her lose what might be only chance to taste him, she eased in and closed her mouth hotly over his pulse. His hands curled around her waist to hold her closer, and when her teeth scraped, his fingers bit in.

The first pierce of her teeth into his skin had his eyes widening with a blend of shock and lust. The erotic storm that whipped through his veins in response to actually *feeling* her drink his blood was stunning in its power. The little purring sound of delight she made went right to his head. He *burned* to take her where they stood. When she finally lifted her head, he dragged her in for a kiss that walked the edge of self-combustion. He could actually taste his blood in her mouth but it didn't bother him. In fact, he barely noticed at all.

What he did notice was the way she began to glow softly. Even in the darkness, she glowed. She was both light and dark. The Gray Etyrnal. He began to truly understand what it meant, and yet he did not care. It was her beautiful heart and impish soul that had the true power.

The clouds parted overhead to let the other moons shine down, and they slowly parted as well. She eased back and lightly touched her lips with her fingers. Her entire body trembled with nearly violent need. "Compatible hormones," she managed to say, and her voice was far huskier than usual. "I really think we need a new term for this."

"I think we're going to be lucky to make it to a bed at this rate," he countered. "Do you know a rain dance?"

She blinked at him and then began giggling. "Is it terrible that I actually understood why you asked?" Her breath hitched as he pulled her into his arms and held on. Somehow, she just felt more *alive* when he was holding her. "Matt."

"Let me hold you." He buried his face in her hair. "I just feel like you need me to hold you."

Maybe she did. She slowly held onto him in return and put her head on his shoulder. She had trouble imagining what her life would be like when he eventually left it. She fell a little more in love with him with every passing minute. They were definitely going need that rain dance to bring in clouds. It might be the only way she could protect him from her deepest desire to keep him by her side always. If she fell too much deeper in love, that desire would override any other—including her desire to give him free will.

Thank the moons there was no such thing as destiny. She would be in a lot more trouble with *that* extra complication on her plate!

Chapter Five

It was cold in the castle. It was always cold. Even in the dead of summer when the shade was scorching. Even when every fireplace was lit and every window was open. Ice clung to the air in a way that chilled the soul while flesh sweated. The deeper through the palace you went, the colder it became. Emotional icicles hung around the throne room and the royal chambers beyond.

Blood had built the current monarchy. A violent, bloody massacre had come three decades before and removed the royal lineage. That lineage had governed Rikan for over three centuries, and in one single night it had disappeared. The king and queen had been murdered in their own bedchamber. The prince and princess had disappeared into the madness, and their bodies had eventually been found among the servants' bodies. Not even the staff had been spared.

The people of the country prayed for peace. They prayed that the ghosts of those who were gone would not rise up and devour them all. Most of all, they prayed for the new king to die. He was old, and he was sick, and his heart had begun to fail him. The doctors claimed he had little time left. Citizen and servant alike prayed that it was true—but only to themselves. Criticizing the king was an instant death sentence.

King Feran paced restlessly in front of his throne with such vigor that he began to cough. He had once been fit enough but illness on top of illness had sapped his strength and made him gaunt. The fit this time seemed to threaten to break his bones.

Darren Richards had been kneeling in the middle of the room and he looked up quickly at the coughing. "My lord?" he asked. The king's face was so red that he half expected him to keel over on the floor. It would certainly make things easier if he did.

"I am fine!" Feran gasped out. He sat down hard on his throne. He wanted immortality. He wanted to rule forever. At this rate, he would not even rule for his natural lifetime. He needed a Greater Runic! Only that could reverse his illness and make him whole. "Report!" he barked.

"I encountered resistance," Darren answered. He kept his gaze obediently on the floor until he was commanded to rise. Even then he did not look at Feran directly. Feran considered it to be offensive, and Darren didn't entirely like looking at him anyway. "As we had suspected, Commander Logan is the Devoted to the Gray Etyrnal herself."

Feran waved a hand dismissively. "A girl."

Darren bit his lip. Anyone who assumed a True Etyrnal over three hundred years old was a 'mere girl' probably deserved to eat the business end of a ghost's rage. "She is powerful regardless. She called for her Dark Etyrnal friends, as I thought she might. She did not hold the line when I threatened fire, though. She retreated to wherever she stashed Logan and the child." He thought about it, then offered, "They will not stay in one place. They will head for Coronia Kingdom. We could intercept them at the towns along the way."

"Already done," Feran told him impatiently. "The moment you said they were in Coronia, I sent out messengers. The sheriff in Truan knows his duty."

"The sheriff?" His brows shot up.

"Money talks, General Richards. Never forget that." Feran sat back on his throne and turned over what he knew. Matthias Logan was the key to getting his hands on something he had been seeking for a long time. The child might also be useful—if she was who he thought she might be. The fact that both were protected by Etyrnals did not concern him. Once he got his hands on them, then he would be Etyrnal himself. He just needed to get to them before his lungs got to him.

Chapter Six

When Matthias awoke the following morning, he was surprised that he had fallen back asleep at all. It was a few hours after dawn and it was still somewhat dim out. He started to get up but realized that his arm was being held down. His eyes opened and he discovered Kae had crawled into his arms and was snuggled up close. Love filled him. This tiny little creature was far more dangerous than any enemy he had ever encountered. She had climbed into his heart before he knew he was in trouble. Perhaps Coronia could help him with an adoption as well.

He gingerly freed himself and sat up. He looked around and did not see either Selene or Niall in sight. Gardina walked into the camp area from deeper in the trees and saw the look on his face. "They're doing a perimeter check and grabbing a nap. They'll be back eventually. Don't worry about them and the sun. S'why they wear cloaks with hoods all the time. Actually, all Etyrnals wear them just in case they get caught in their bad time."

"Unlike you who can wear whatever she wants."

"Yep." She sat down beside the fire and leaned

back on her hands. "I'm preternaturally tidy so I can get away with wearing white. Besides, dark colors just wash me out entirely. Vlad stuck me in his cloak once." She snorted. "Other than the fact that it was just entirely too big, it was one of the few times where I looked more dead than alive. I normally straddle the line quite well."

"Not that you *encourage* people to think you're a ghost."

"Mortals amuse me. I can't help it." She shot him an impish grin. "If it makes you feel better, I even got Niall with that when I first met him. Selene hadn't told him about me. I just couldn't resist!"

It definitely made him feel better to think the rough and tough Dark Etyrnal had been spooked at one point. He scooted closer to where she was sitting and skimmed his fingers through her hair. She looked up at him a bit warily and he smiled. "I just needed to touch you. I keep worrying that I've dreamed you up."

"I admit things have gotten interesting." She shook her head. "Each time I think it can't get more complicated, it does." She drew her knees up and lightly wrapped her arms around them. "Thank you," she added softer, "for last night."

A corner of his lips kicked up. "I think we both

know I enjoyed myself."

"Not *that*. For being there. For holding me."

He studied her. "How long had it been since anyone held you, Gardina?"

"About seventy years, give or take a few, but it wasn't quite the same thing." She looked up at him with a wry smile. "I've had a few lovers in my lifetime, but it was always very casual. If something bothered me, I kept it to myself. They never pushed to know."

"Then you've been with idiots."

She blinked, then giggled softly. "Matthias, are we a smidge jealous?"

"No," he muttered.

"Liar."

He sighed. "Fine, I'm a bit jealous. It's an irrational emotion when you're three centuries old, and I know that, but I think being a Devoted makes me as possessive and protective of you as it makes you of me."

She leaned over and lightly kissed his chin. "I'm not bothered by any of your past relationships, you know."

"There's only one to be bothered by," he groused. "I've never had much free time over my life, and let's be fair. Who wants to be in a relationship—of any kind—with someone likely to be killed on a battlefield?"

Most soldiers remained single until wartime ended. She had been noticing the phenomena for three centuries. Perhaps blessedly for soldiers, wars were often short enough to make being alone tolerable. The war currently underway was far from normal. "I don't mind your lack of experience." Her eyes twinkled. "I don't mind teaching you a few things, though I'd say you had things well enough in hand last night."

That was his clue to change the subject—the Ghost Moon was cheerfully in the clear sky—and he was rescued by Kae beginning to stir. He leaned over and scooped her up onto his lap. She snuggled closer and yawned sleepily as she opened her eyes a bit. "S'morning?"

"It is. Sleep well?"

"Uh-huh." She rubbed at her eyes. "Can we make a house?"

He found himself bemused as he realized that he understood her logic: a house meant a bedroom which meant a bed, and she was tired of sleeping on the ground. Even without the direct conscious link, he could still essentially read and understand her thoughts if they were strong enough, and vice-versa. "Someday soon," he promised. He rubbed his thumb over her upper arm where it seemed as if her family mark might be starting to change.

Gardina had already noticed the shift. Kae had made her choice about what she wanted to happen in her future. It wouldn't cement and become formal until the adoption was finalized, and Matthias would also discover his mark returning in the same shape. Her eyes lowered to where she could see the faint residue of his former mark on his lower arm. "What happened to your family?" she asked.

"My parents were servants in the Rikan royal house," he admitted. "When Feran staged the coup, he erased *everyone*. No one was spared. I was one of maybe five escapees. I barely remember the events at all; I was about three or so at the time. I went into the orphanage with another boy. He was adopted quickly, but I wasn't. At thirteen, I enlisted in the army to get out of the orphanage."

"And you took to it quickly," she murmured.

"Mmm. Had a natural skill. I've been in the army since. Promoted to Commander of the Armed Forces about five years ago. Probably should've been General already, but, well." He shrugged. "I'm surprised Feran even allowed me to promote as high as I did. Guess it has to do with whatever reason they're now hunting me. Maybe they think my connection to the original lineage would be what turned me traitor. There isn't even a lineage *left*."

"There are a lot of loose threads in this," she muttered. "I feel like you're at the center of things."

"But *how*?"

"I don't know!" she exclaimed in exasperation. "If I did, we sure as heck wouldn't be just sitting here twiddling our thumbs!"

"What's a twiddle?"

Gardina blinked at Kae. "Uhm. Huh." She squinted one eye as she thought about it but finally gave up and just showed her the gesture. "This. A useless gesture where we're not going anywhere and doing nothing."

"Oh." She accepted that and looked around. "Where're Niall and Selene?"

"Not far away. They're snagging a quick nap before they take you somewhere safe."

Kae's eyes went wide and she scrambled off Matthias' lap. "No!" she shouted. "I don't want to go with them! I want to go with you!"

"You have to," Matthias noted mildly. "It's for your safety."

"No! No, no, no!" Her hands clenched into fists at her sides. Blue power rippled over her body and was echoed by thunder overhead. "You won't come back for me! No one ever comes back!"

"Kae." Gardina's voice was very soft. "Turn it off."

"You're not my mom!" the girl shot at her.

"I am your future Runic Trainer, and that's far different. If you want to be a Runic Master, you need a trainer. I am a True Etyrnal. I can help you master whatever you may choose to wield." She neither stood nor moved from her casual position, and yet she seemed to radiate something nearly royal. "Stand down, apprentice."

Kae stared at her for a long moment and then crossed her arms and stopped glowing. A sulky expression settled over her features as the threatening clouds dissipated before they fully formed. Matthias couldn't help but let out a little breath of relief. Trying to deal with a storm every time his temperamental daughter lost said temper would *not* be fun.

"Come here." Gardina held out a hand with a

smile. Kae crossed to her, and she tugged her down for a snuggle. "I know it's hard to control your power when you're new to it, let alone when you're young. I had a lot of snags when I got my Runic. Selene could tell you tales. Eventually, you'll get the hang of things, and starting this young is a good thing for you. It will let you reach a higher level in the end."

"I love you, Ghosty!" Kae hugged her fiercely for a long moment. She then let her go and rushed over to throw her arms around Matthias instead. "I'm sorry, Matt!" She eased back and her lower lip quivered. "Can I call you 'Daddy'? Can you adopt me?"

"Yes to the first, but not yet to the second." He smoothed her hair back. "Once Gardina and I remove the danger, I can adopt you. I don't want him to think you're important to me. I'm hoping you're not as interesting to them as I am. You go with Selene and Niall for now, and when it's safe, I'll come back for you. I absolutely promise."

It was likely that separating them would keep Kae out of Feran and Richards' sight. If they wanted her for her half-Fae blood, they might still try to go after her, but they wouldn't be able to spare the manpower to pursue her *and* Matthias at the same time, and he was the bigger target. The surveillance and previous pursuit alone proved it. Gardina was still tempted to just go erase the problem, but that wouldn't give them answers *why*.

She was diverted from her thoughts when Kae looked at her and said very seriously, "Can you marry my dad so you're my mommy?"

A hint of pink climbed Gardina's neck. "Uhm." How in the name of the moons did she answer *that*? Her relationship with Matthias was too complicated to explain to a seven-year-old. They were inevitable lovers, and there was a high likelihood of him becoming an Etyrnal as well, if only because she wouldn't be able to stop herself from changing him. And, yeah, she was smart enough to know that if *she* was in love, then he was going to be in love with her eventually as well. That was how it worked.

Matthias tried to hide a smile at the look on her face. Deciding to take pity on her, he told Kae, "How about breakfast?"

Kae's empty stomach overrode her desire to get a promise of staying around out of her future mom. "Okay!"

If only adults could be so easily diverted. Gardina just shook her head and grabbed the sack of berries and nuts she had hunted down that morning.

She divvied out portions for Matthias and Kae alike, and when they eyed her empty hands curiously, she smiled. "Etyrnals don't *have* to eat food unless we want to. I technically already had my breakfast."

The look she shot Matthias was more than a bit sultry and wholly impish. The combination clenched his heart and heated his blood. He quickly popped a berry in his mouth before he said something he regretted. The fact that he could *feel* where she had bitten him—though the mark had faded—was not helping. It still tingled and tormented his nerves.

Kae intently eyed the odd nut she was holding and tried carefully to bite into the shell. There was no give, and the shell tasted terrible. "It's broken," she announced.

"No, it's not," Gardina countered dryly. She chucked the nut into the fire and it popped open with a small cracking noise. The inner nut flipped up into the air and she caught it on the way back. "See? You can also smash the outer shell, but this is the fun way."

"I've never had these before," Matthias noted. He chucked a nut into the fire and found himself grinning when it promptly spit the edible part back out. "Okay, this *is* fun."

Gardina watched him and Kae happily crack open the nuts and realized anew what her ethereal companion had meant by saying she brought innocence into Matthias' life. He didn't even know about chomper nuts. *All* kids knew about them. Kae was roughly the right age to encounter them for the first time, but Matthias was long overdue. What else had he missed out on by living in an orphanage and then enlisting in the army so young?

Her eyes widened as she saw him palm a handful of nuts. "Wait!" she blurted.

She was too late. He chucked the handful in, and they promptly started exploding. She hastily went translucent and he grabbed Kae to shield her with his body. The shrapnel eventually died, and he looked at Gardina with such wide-eyed disbelief that she fell over with the giggles. "Everyone does that!" she managed to say between peals. "Every kid does that! My dad once swore I and my sister were trying to give him and our mother a heart attack!"

A hint of pink climbed Matthias' face but he couldn't resent his, apparently, childish action since it had made her so happy. Laughter brought a fresh flush of life to her face that made her radiantly beautiful. "Glad I could amuse you," he groused.

She straightened

up with the impish grin that never failed to grab his heart. "Did you know that someone once, seriously, tried to use chompers as a weapon? The cannons were out of ammo, and all they had were sacks of nuts sitting around."

Kae's eyes went wide. "Did it work?"

"Depends on who you ask. The people using it said it was ineffective. The people getting pelted by chompers said it was a contributing factor to them retreating. Can you imagine the royal news reporting that? *Death by nuts.*" She grabbed the basket of berries sitting nearby and said, "And because I like you both, I'll save you from another childhood folly. Piper Berries. Don't eat them whole! Pull out the stem and soak them in your cups of water first. It will leech out the spiciness."

Neither father nor daughter had any desire to see just how spicy the berries might taste. They dunked them in water and ate them that way. The surprising sweetness seemed deceptive when they were rumored to be naturally spicy. "Can you cook with them?" Matthias asked curiously. "Safely? And without intending to torment your friends or family?"

She giggled. "Yes, you can!" She sighed gustily with memory. "The royal chef used to make a pudding from Piper Berries that was so rich and decadent that we only had it on special occasions."

"*Royal* chef?" he asked softly.

She hastily shut her mouth. She had not intended to let that slip. Rather than try to make up an excuse or lie, she said nothing at all. She preferred to keep her status as a princess quiet. The truth was . . . she was technically the rightful monarch of Coronia. The current king was her nephew many times removed. Her family had tried to insist she could still be queen, and certainly Selene had tried to convince her in the time since, but she just didn't feel like ruling anything except her own life. Every subsequent generation of her lineage had told her the same thing: change your mind, and the throne is yours.

Matthias watched her walk into the trees and frowned thoughtfully. He had already assumed she was connected to the royal family because of the manor, but now he was even more curious. He wanted to know everything about her. All of her history and her origins. He didn't want there to be any secrets left between them.

He scraped a hand over his face with a sigh. He was ready to give up the fight. He had to be in love. *In* love. He really couldn't imagine there being any other explanation for the way he felt about Gardina. The desire was only a small portion of the jumble of hungry emotions inside him. Once they were on their journey and they had some real privacy, they needed to talk. If she could transform him, then he wanted her to do it. He wanted that eternity promised to them. It promised to be as sweet and spicy as the infamous Piper Berries. And if transformation might be too dangerous until after they took care of Richards, well, then they would just wait. The Ghost Moon would return to the sky next year if they missed it this year.

The sheer fact that he was making a decision that would change his life, and he didn't at all feel afraid or unnerved by it, told him he was making the right one. Whichever of the gods had decided to make him her Devoted deserved a medal. Not that he would tell *her* that.

"Daddy?"

He blinked and looked at Kae. "Yes?" Bemused, he added, "I thought that might take getting used to, but it feels nice." Just another decision he could not regret. It was time he started taking control of his life, and reaching for the things he wanted to keep close. A family. It was such a beautiful concept. "What's wrong?"

"I want a bath!" She scowled. "I'm dirty and itchy and my clothes are too big!"

Considering her clothes consisted of a hastily altered tunic belonging to Gardina, it was no wonder. "We can't do anything about any of that right now," he sighed, "but I'm sure Selene and Niall can get you cleaned up and into fresh clothes once you're safely hidden away." He couldn't help but smirk at the idea of Niall taking the tiny half-Fae shopping. To be a fly on the wall for that!

An otherworldly cry rose on the air that made both Kae and Matthias' skin crawl. She scrambled over to him and burrowed into his arms for safety. He held her tighter and bitterly wished for his now demolished sword and gun. Both had been destroyed in the arson.

A soft, feminine touch swept across his mind. *I am here*, Gardina's voice whispered gently in his ears alone. Her hands settled on his shoulders and he looked up swiftly to see she was really there. She had gone translucent again though he did still feel her touch. He had no idea how she was doing it, and he didn't really care. Her normally gentle and smiling face had gone very still and cool. In that moment, he could believe she was as Dark as she was Light.

Something wispy and misshapen emerged from the trees as it continued to cry its mournful song. There was no determining who or what it had once been. The face had distorted and blurred and not even gender could be determined on its oddly formed shell. A ghost. Matthias knew it for what it was though he had never seen one other than Gardina. Her ability to retain her figure underscored her power.

The ghost spotted them and gave an eerie shriek as it shot toward Matthias and Kae alike. Though fast, it was not intelligent. It tried to go through the fire and was only engulfed in flames for its efforts. Its shrieks rose in volume and Matthias covered his ears as he ducked down and tried to shelter Kae more. He felt oddly sick to his stomach.

Gardina was eternally calm. She lightly touched her Runic symbol and began to speak words that had no meaning. The shrieks were cut off abruptly as the ghost dissolved entirely into streamers of silvery-green color that dissipated in the sunlight. Silence descended. After a moment, Matthias straightened up. Kae was trembling but she bravely asked, "What was that?"

"Old news." Gardina's voice was somehow

both neutral and weary. She shook it off and became solid again as she knelt beside Matthias. "Are you alright?" she asked. She pressed a cool hand to his forehead. "Ghost shrieks can immobilize people entirely."

"I feel slightly queasy but otherwise fit." He shook it off. "What brought that on?"

"Meh, hard to say." She sat down with a sigh. "Probably a dose of jealousy. It had lost so much of its self that it wanted only to take back what it had lost. Whether it was after you or Kae is debatable. It would have gone after anyone it encountered."

Sensing her desire to not discuss it, he shelved it for something else to talk about later. "You do know you can't keep just walking away from my questions or changing the subject to get out of talking about something, right?"

She sighed gustily. "I'm beginning to think you don't trust me, Matt." She gave him a solemn look entirely ruined by the mischievous light in her eyes. "I don't think this relationship is working out. We should see other people."

He looked at Kae. "Get her."

Kae promptly clambered over onto Gardina's lap and held on tight. "You can't dump Daddy!" she announced. "Not until, uhm, you date for at least a month." Surely a month would give her time to figure out how to get Gardina for a mommy. "Okay? A month?" She brightened. "Wait! You can't break up until Daddy officially adopts me because you have to help him, okay?"

"Your child," Gardina groused at Matthias.

"I already dread her as a teenager," he groused back. It was neither the time nor place to lay bare his heart and beg her to let him stay with her forever, but he wanted to at least put the thought in her head. He reached out and cupped her chin. "Gardina," he said very softly, "I want far, *far* more than a month with you."

A potent blend of emotions stole her voice, churned up desire, clenched her heart, and even made her incisors lengthen against her will at the memory of his taste. If it hadn't been for the little girl cuddling her, she would have grabbed onto her Devoted with all of her strength and never let go again. Eternity. He wanted it with her. It felt, almost, like a miracle.

Watching from the trees, Selene felt her lips tremble as she fought back her own emotions. Niall's arms slid around her waist and she turned to hold onto him. She had *prayed*. She had prayed for *years* that Gardina might someday find happiness. She had spent too many years banishing the spirits of the deceased—including her own family members, like the one just passed. With every passing year, Selene had been sure she would eventually choose to live entirely in the world of the dead.

Matthias had brought her back to life. The gods had listened to Selene's prayers. Now she and Niall just needed to make sure that everyone involved survived long enough to enjoy a happy ending. They would do their part by protecting Kae, but if Gardina and Matthias needed them for anything, all bets would be off.

Chapter Seven

"Good mornin'," Niall said as he and Selene came out of the trees to join the small family. He grinned when Kae waved cheerfully at him. "Hello to you too, little mite." He scooped her up when she ran over and then passed her along to Selene. He spotted Gardina and Matthias mutually eyeing him and Selene and shook his head. "Don't you worry none. We're tired, to be sure, but we can sleep plenty later." He smirked at Matthias. "We won't be burstin' into flames. That's a myth, friend."

"I'm more worried about you passing out," was the retort.

"Now, boys." Gardina held up her hands. "Let's play nice. Sheesh." She was reluctantly resigned to a future filled with bickering like this. No matter how close the two males might end up, they would still snipe at each other. It was simply their personalities at work. She would have to call Vlad in to be the voice of reason.

Niall shook his head at her. "You wouldn't know what t'do with me if I was nice." He crossed his arms. "Y'all might want to start out soon. The sun don't hurt Ghosty none, but that won't make it any less uncomfortable for you to travel in, Matt. Even Coronia can get hot this time of year, and you'll be leavin' the forest on your way to Truan."

"It's a day or two," Gardina offered to Matthias as well. "If we start now, we'll get there by tomorrow afternoon." She huffed out a quick breath. "I'd feel so much better about this if you were armed," she told her Devoted. "Even with a Runic of some kind."

Niall removed the holster he was wearing and offered it and the gun within to Matthias. "You can use mine for now. I expect you to return it later."

It was a subtle statement of confidence, and Matthias accepted it along with the weapon. His eyes met the older male's. "If things go right, I might have different weapons of my own shortly."

A smile softened Niall's face. "Good to hear. Now get out of here. We'll head the other way."

Kae held out her arms demandingly, and Matthias took her for a quick cuddle. It would be an odd thing to not have her around either in his mind or his life. She had become a valuable part of his existence in a very short time. Strange how that worked. It also clenched his heart to see Gardina snuggle Kae as well. His family. His miracle.

They parted ways shortly thereafter. Gardina and Matthias made their way back toward the ruins of the manor and then turned north. It took only an hour or two of following shortcuts before they emerged from the forest and into the start of farmland. It was indeed getting warm, but the crops were thriving. Coronia hadn't bothered to fight against the land the way the other two countries had; they had learned to work with it.

The primary export was wheat, one of the biggest staples of most diets. Matthias studied the landscape and thoughtfully asked, "Shouldn't this part of the land belong to the manor?"

"It did once," she agreed amiably. She didn't mind so much anymore, answering his questions. Knowing he wanted to be her future made it easier to look back at the past. "Once the manor became a royal retreat, the land itself was given over to other farmers." She lifted from the ground and floated along beside him.

"You want to get into how you got your hands on a royal retreat?"

Her smile turned a bit impish. "I'm not sure you'll like the answer."

"Do try."

"Okay. How's it feel to be a commoner associating with a crown princess?"

A corner of his mouth kicked up. "Surprisingly comfortable. And I'll admit that I'm not too surprised by that. It had been in the back of my mind ever since I learned you had the Ghost Runic. Everyone knows it belonged to the Coronia royal house and was 'lost with the death of a monarch' three centuries ago. You have said Runic and you're, surprise, over three centuries in age."

"I'm surprised more people haven't made the connection," she admitted dryly.

"Technically, doesn't being the *crown* princess mean you're supposed to be in charge?"

"Technically." She linked her hands behind her back on a sigh. "The current king is my great-great-great-great-great nephew. Descendant of my little sister. My family insisted there would be nothing wrong with me being an Etyrnal and being queen, that I could simply adopt a child should I ever want an heir, but I just . . ."

"Didn't feel as if you belonged in the land of the living." He skimmed a finger down her cheek when she looked at him in surprise. "I think I've come to understand you very well, Ghosty."

His use of her nickname warmed her through to her soul. "I'm not that complicated, you know. Emotionally." She smiled. "If I love, I love. If I dislike, I dislike. Can't say that I hate because I can't hate anything—okay, I hate certain foods, but that's different. If I want to cry, I do. Being an adult doesn't mean giving up what defines us as children. It just means experiencing everything *more*."

"I was never really a child," he murmured.

"That's why you need me." She slipped her hand into his. "You need me to give you back the things you were cheated out of having. I need you to—to remind me that I am alive." The last was admitted in a rush for she had only just begun to understand what her silver-haired companion had been implying.

That was his cue. "Gardina." He stopped walking and turned her to face him. "I want to say it right out." He cupped her face in his hands. "In my darkest moment, you saved my sanity. Somewhere between death and life, madness and sanity, you found me. I'm not honestly sure I ever *fell* in love with you. I just know I am. I want to be an Etyrnal. I want to share your eternity."

Tears shimmered across her golden eyes as she looked up at him. "You just want a mother for your kid so you don't have to deal with puberty."

Humor darkened his eyes to a rich verdant green. It was a strangely familiar color to her, now that she was looking closer, though she couldn't peg why. "I won't deny that I'd be very glad to have you handle that," he said dryly, "but I'd feel this way with or without her in my life. I think from the moment I was born that this was inevitable. Let me love you, Ghosty. Love me in return. We can have a family of our own."

Nature, destiny, or coincidence. She kind of didn't really care anymore what force was at play. "I'm really, really glad you feel the way I do," she admitted in a rush. "I was getting so afraid that I might take your choice away!" Her lips trembled. "Logic said that if I was in love that you would have to be, too, but logic means nothing when your heart and soul are involved. I didn't know how long I'd keep from trying to convert you! The deeper I fell, the more I wanted you to be with me always!"

"Even if I hadn't consciously made this choice," he promised, "I would have accepted the consequences. It's been on my mind all along." He smiled. "I'm a Devoted, remember? We usually become Etyrnals anyway, or so I was told. It would be hard to resent that."

She winced. "You'd be surprised, actually." She rose up off the ground and wound her arms around his neck. "You'll need at least a few hours of uninterrupted sleep after being transformed. Day or night, doesn't matter, since you'll be Gray like me. You will need absolute dark, though. Etyrnals can't sleep in *any* type of light; even Light Etyrnals can't do it. Your current level of health or age will determine how much recovery time you need. You being healthy, whole, and young means you'd probably bounce back quickly."

"How did it happen for you?"

She hesitated. "Can we discuss that later? It's not comfortable to remember, and I think you might be a smidge upset by it. Remember, I'm a bit of an aberration. I promise to tell you eventually. I *will* say that it was traumatic and it was almost an entire day before I woke."

"Fair enough." He kissed her lightly and lingered for a moment to savor her taste. "Once we can find a place where we can rest safely," he murmured huskily against her lips, "I will very happily put myself into your capable hands for anything."

She giggled. "Truan has a very nice inn. No one would dare bother us there. The people who see me treat me warily since they know I own the manor." She nipped at his lower lip and let him feel the edge of her sharp teeth. The way his hands tightened was thrilling. "I have a lot to teach you," she murmured huskily. "It's going to be fun."

They continued along on their way, and she kept him entertained with some of the tales of her life. She had done quite a bit over three centuries. He looked forward to spending the next few, and many more, with her.

When they were forced to camp for the night, they did so in a campsite specifically designed for such a thing. It was off the beaten trail and tucked between two farms. They argued very briefly over who would stand guard, though. She argued that she couldn't sleep in any light and therefore might as well guard, and he argued that she hadn't sleep in two days already.

They finally compromised by him staying up the first half of the night while she tried to sleep wrapped up inside his jacket. Her restless turning got him, though, and he eventually laid down and tugged her into his arms. He more fully covered her head and face, and she finally settled in. He was half-tempted to not wake her at all but suspected he didn't want to learn if she had a temper.

He lightly drifted off for a few moments thanks to her peaceful breathing, but he woke quickly when he sensed another presence. He held Gardina closer with one arm and slowly reached for his gun with the other. A shimmer of color caught his eye and he looked sharply to the side. There he found an insubstantial figure that didn't wholly resemble a ghost and yet didn't look alive, either.

He was relatively easily to distinguish characteristics on, and his face was unknown. His aura wavered in a strangely familiar way, though Matthias didn't recall ever seeing auras of anyone before. The figure looked at him for several moments and then heaved a sigh and disappeared.

After the strange events recently passed, Matthias barely rated that as a two. He put his gun back and settled in for the rest of the night. He obligingly woke Gardina at midnight to let her take over things, and he pulled his jacket over his head instead. Perhaps as a sign of his future life, he had never really liked sleeping with any light around, either.

He woke with the dawn, a bit grudgingly, and didn't argue when she fed him the fruit she had fetched from a nearby orchard. He also didn't argue when he noticed that she had the faint glow meaning she had fed herself somewhere else. "I don't mind," he groused. "I won't be of any use to you after you transform me, you know." He blinked. "Or will I?"

She patted his cheek with a smile. "I refrained this morning because I *really* don't trust myself— you're really bitable—and you technically will still be 'of use' to me after transformation just as I would be to you. Etyrnals can feed each other just fine so long as someone at some point is eating externally. The internal cycle of power would get murky otherwise."

He cocked his head. "Would I be limited to fresh blood like you or would I be more like Selene and Niall?"

"Probably them. It's my Runic messing me up. It's not fused to me the way Runics normally are. It's part of the long story I owe you later." Her eyes twinkled with humor. "Basically, you could drink bottled blood and then turn around and feed me. It's probably the safe route for us to go, anyway. You're already magically potent without making you an Etyrnal. And it'll keep you from being jealous."

"I can't control that," he muttered. "And expect me to sink my teeth into you as well. It's already pretty tempting."

She giggled. "Always a sign of a Devoted on the cusp. Your instincts are already stirring and prepping you. I should've been expecting your decision already," she had to admit. "You showed one of the big preparation points already. You kissed me after I had fed on you, and you didn't recoil at the taste of blood."

"I barely noticed it at all."

"Wait until you find you *like* it. That unnerves more than a few at first." She snorted. "I'm not ashamed to say that Selene spent a week laughing at me because I jumped every time I felt my incisors grow and I complained each time I realized how much I liked the taste of blood. It's *weird* to change species overnight. I kinda wish I'd been a Devoted so I could be prepared for it myself!"

He had no doubt he would entertain her as well, but he was fine with that. He was just glad that the gods gave him the chance to adjust at all. "Well, tell me about Truan," he offered. "Since we're only a few hours out."

"Truan is pretty nice all things considered. Relatively decent sized and they have a big trading hub since they're right near farmlands. They're a bit out of the way as far as cities in Coronia go, but that's mostly because most cities were built clustered together near the castle. The capitol city, with said castle, is right along the ocean and so that's where the biggest trade with the rest of the world comes from."

"Small but powerful," he decided. "I don't recall Desertia or Rikan ever trying to take Coronia though they've spat with each other for ages, even before Feran instigated full-scale war over a Greater Runic." He added in a mutter, "Maybe if he hadn't murdered everyone in the Rikan royal house, he might have had a chance at finding the Sovereign."

"I'm still not convinced that's not *why* he staged the coup." She shrugged. "As for the reason why Coronia has stayed neutral, it's because we're kinda valuable to the other two countries. Actually, way back, there was intent to have an alliance between Rikan and Coronia via a royal marriage. It was to be followed by one between Coronia and Desertia as well. Basically force everyone to play nice."

"Perchance was your marriage to be one of them?"

"Yep. Another chunk of the long story. I've always thought that eventually another chance might come to get the three countries unified via family ties if we can just get everyone to sit down and talk rather than fight."

Her innocent ability to believe in the greater good, and a world that didn't need war, was strangely humbling and endearing. He wanted to believe what she did, but it was hard. He had seen too much battle already. It never took much to set it off. How could anything end it?

Proving again to be able to read his mind, she said softly, "Matt, do you honestly believe an entire country wants a war? *Leaders* want a war. If we can replace dominating, greedy leaders with ones willing to talk and listen, then there will be no war. At this point, frankly, just getting rid of Feran would make things better. Until he came around, Desertia and Rikan were

"Ah, so it was before Desertia got the Greater Water Runic." always like, I don't know, stepkids or something. They would kick and throw things but never really disliked each other." She suddenly giggled. "Coronia would send them to their rooms without dessert if they got too bad."

It made him laugh as well. "So tell me about Coronia, then. How did the Campbell family come to be the ruling house?"

"We kind of made the country. It was, hmm, about two centuries before my birth. Desertia and Rikan were already around and, of course, shooting spitballs at each other over this unused chunk of land between them. At the time, Desertia had no greenery, and Rikan had already chopped down most of its forests."

"Yup. My ancestor decided that the easiest way to end the bickering was to just claim it for himself. He moved himself and his wife and kids out, and they started building the castle. Since the land wasn't owned, no one could tell him not to do it." She grinned. "The other two lands kinda pitched a fit, but couldn't say nothing. They stomped and sulked the entire time the castle got built, and people started migrating in to form a city as well. My ancestor finished the castle, crowned himself king, and declared a democracy known as Coronia."

"That . . . that isn't how it works . . ."

She started giggling anew. "The people said that too! They told him that if he wanted a castle and a crown, he had to be a danged king and rule a monarchy. He proved to be pretty darn good at it! His eldest daughter inherited and was a good queen, and then her son, and the people decided the Campbells should stay as long as possible. Our neighboring countries groused some more but eventually gave up and decided they had been beat."

"And Desertia then found the Water Runic and didn't need the new land."

"Precisely. It was followed by Rikan finding the Sovereign Runic and using it to increase trade with other lands. My family found the Ghost Runic but never used it. It was just a royal treasure until not long before I was born. It was lost in a remodeling project and no one knew where it had gone until I found it."

"Or it found you," he murmured.

"It is debatable," she admitted. "Only a Campbell could use it, so perhaps it was drawn to my blood."

"If no one ever wore it, how could it be attached to your family?"

"I genuinely don't know. It just was." She smiled. "Runics are strange and powerful things. I've always thought mine had a spirit. Maybe it just knew eventually it would find a good wielder in my family."

"That sounds suspiciously like a belief in destiny, my little non-believer."

"Nah, destiny would be me believing that I alone was meant to be its user and that everything that has happened thus far was meant to. I've made too many conscious choices to believe that kind of junk."

He had a feeling her ancestor wasn't the only slightly oxymoronic one, but he let it slide. "Desertia said they lost the Water Runic," he murmured, "but Feran didn't believe them because the land was still lush."

"The Runic *is* lost, but the effects will last forever," she confirmed. "It disappeared about two years ago, right before the crown prince decided to abdicate his right to the throne and raise his family in a normal city. He figured the missing Runic was a sign that it was time for a change. His mother still rules; when either she passes away or she chooses to hand off duties, her younger son will take over." She cocked her head as she remembered something else. "Actually, the crown prince and his wife died a year ago. They had a daughter, I think. She might grow up and make a bid for the throne if she wants."

"I still feel like we're missing something in this entire scenario," he sighed. "Feran wants a Runic to be an Etyrnal. That's easy to figure out. The minute you said it could make someone young again, I figured that was his intent. He's old and frail, and getting worse daily. But why spy on me? And why the interest in Kae? Her half-Fae blood?"

"I have . . . suspicions about Kae," she said softly. "Things I keep silent on because I might be wrong. As for you, I genuinely don't know. It might have something to do with you surviving the coup. Maybe you know something you don't know you know. You said you don't remember anything, right? Maybe there's something you *should* remember."

"I'm beginning to want to encounter Richards," he muttered. "I have some questions for him."

"You and me both!"

It was closer to evening than afternoon when they finally entered the city limits. It was well populated for being out of the way, and the businesses were still busy at that time of day. It did not take long for Matthias to finally make sense of what Gardina had said before about 'the people who saw her.' Somehow, strangely, she seemed invisible to most of the people they passed. They literally did not see her at all. The kids certainly did, and they ran up with happy smiles, but a great deal of adults did not.

"Not many adults see me," she murmured as she drifted along at his side. "Someone recently said I represented the innocence lost to adults. I suppose we shall see if it's just me, or if it has to do with being Gray." She smiled up at him. "When you are Gray as well, we will have to see if adults stop seeing you."

He didn't mind whichever it turned out to be, but his heart ached anew for her. She had been far, far too alone. No wonder she had trouble remembering she was alive. He glanced down the road and the corner of his lips kicked up into a lethal smile. "I see an inn. Be gentle with me."

Her counter smile was teasing and anticipatory. "I always liked dessert in bed." Her entire body suddenly went still and her eyes narrowed. The way her lover froze as well told her that his wartime instincts had not blunted by being off a battlefield. Danger was approaching. It wasn't Richards, though. It didn't carry his scent.

Matthias grabbed Gardina and yanked her into a side alley moments before bullets sprayed the ground near where they had stood. Amid yelps of civilians rushing for cover, Matthias shifted his body enough to see a reflection of the street in a window. His blood chilled. It was the city's own law enforcement that had shot at them. The male in the front even wore the familiar crown pin that marked him as being the sheriff.

Gardina was not a happy princess. She would have a few words with her nephew and make him call a do-over on the law in Truan. "Someone bought off the sheriff," she muttered. "He has no other reason to target you. You're not identifiable as being from Rikan, and Coronia isn't involved in the war anyway. Both sides can enter our land if they're being peaceful."

"I don't think he knows you're with me. Is he one who can't see you? Can you force yourself to be seen?"

"Yes to both, and my invisibility isn't wholly that. I'm, well, a *ghost* at the corner of their eye. Best that I hide myself entirely and we see if we can't figure out what's going on. Maybe Sheriff Jin knows something about why you're being pursued. I mean, they probably had to tell him something when they handed over the money. He'd need to have an excuse to give the people short of 'I don't like his haircut' or whatever."

"How do you intend to hide yourself?" He

blinked as she suddenly went wholly translucent as she had been the day he had formally met her. "Ghosty?"

She smiled. "I'm going to possess you. It might feel funny because you'll actually be able to feel me inside you, but I promise it won't be dangerous to either of us. Possessing people is actually how I heal them, but they have to be conscious for it to work, hence why I couldn't do anything for Kae."

He nodded. "Go for it. And hurry. We're running out of time." His eyes widened as she wrapped her arms around him and then seemed to simply disappear entirely. Moments later, he felt her inside his blood and soul equally. It was a shockingly intimate sensation that only briefly startled him. Somehow, feeling her that close helped fill his ever-present craving to make love to her. Perhaps, in a way, it was much the same. He looked forward to finding out, providing they survived.

"Come out with your hands visible, Commander Logan!"

"Can I be guaranteed you won't immediately shoot me down?" he retorted.

"You're not of any use to us dead!"

Reassuring, but also not comfortable. He held

his hands up and stepped out of the alley. "I hadn't heard the welcome wagon in Coronia was quite so unwelcoming." He saw people glance at him with curiosity for the hint of accent he possessed, but there was more confusion over the entire scene than anything else. "Mind if I ask what the problem is? I'm just passing through."

"We have questions for you." Jin walked over and yanked his arms down to snap on a pair of cuffs. "Let's go, Logan. And no funny business. Where's your Etyrnal pal?"

"Haven't seen her lately." He lifted a brow. "You do realize she'll have your head if you harm me, right? She claims me as her Devoted. I doubt Feran or Richards paid you enough to risk the wrath of a ghost."

All he got for his effort was a sharp smack in the head with the butt of a gun. The throbbing pain barely took hold before he felt a tender and cool touch move through the hurt area. The pain dissipated immediately. A sensation of being hugged surrounded him, and he felt his nerves ease. He really was going to have to find a way to pay Gardina back.

Through his mind, her voice murmured

warmly, *Just snuggle me at night, and we're even. I like how you hold me.*

Jin hauled him into an office and shoved him into a chair. Matthias glanced around the room and immediately noticed that the paint was fresh, the furniture expensive, and the carpet brand new. A sardonic smile touched his lips. How blasé. Accepting blood money to redecorate. "Is this a friendly chat, or do you have a reason for arresting me?" he asked coolly. "I've committed no crimes, and if Rikan has a bounty on my head, it is inapplicable in Coronia as a war-neutral party."

"Just shut up and answer my questions."

"Start asking them, and maybe I will."

Jin seethed and snapped back another retort. Interrogating a normal soldier would be difficult enough, let alone a man who should have been a general. Breaking his will was out of the question. Torturing him would only bring down the wrath of the Etyrnals. Jin wanted to *live* to spend the rest of his money. "What do you know about the Runic?"

Matthias eyed him oddly. "Which Runic? The Ghost Runic?"

"Don't play dumb! I'm talking about the Greater Sovereign Runic!" He slammed his hands onto the desk and made papers jump. "Where did you hide it?"

Genuinely astonished, Matthias stared at him. "I haven't seen it in my life." Something finally clicked, however. *That* was why Feran was watching him! He was probably watching all of the former servants in the hopes of one of them finding the Runic. Perhaps he had mistaken Matthias' Etyrnal Sensitivity as a Devoted for a sign he had the Runic. "I honestly have no idea where it is, what it looks like, or what happened to it. You think I'd be blithely sitting on it after all this? I'd use it to barter my freedom. I've lost interest in war."

Jin glared at him. He had always been able to tell if someone was lying, and Logan's words smacked of the truth. Yet Feran had been *sure* that Logan knew something. If it was buried in Logan's childhood, then perhaps a little *enforced persuasion* would rattle out the memories. He rang a bell on his desk, and when a deputy opened the door, he ordered, "Lock him up. A few days in the dark without any food will soften up his mind."

Matthias said nothing as he was escorted to a cement cell, and he didn't argue as he was uncuffed and shoved inside. The pitch black of the cell after the door shut was not at all bothersome. In fact, it was rather pleasant and made him want a nap. He felt Gardina stir inside and then she left his body and began to emit a glow that allowed him to see. He quirked a brow. "Prep point?"

"Prep point," she agreed. Her even voice was at odds with the darkened intensity of her eyes. "Looks like we delay your transformation a tiny bit. We're not staying in this town. Richards probably already knows we're here. We need to get to a safe spot where we can get some *real* rest without interruption. At this point, transforming you has more to do with keeping you alive than our future." She scowled. "We won't have a future if they try to starve you into a traumatic state where prior trauma might rattle out memories!"

"I don't disagree." He lifted a brow as she headed for the door. "Where are you going?"

"Hunting."

It did not take long before he heard the scrape of a key and the cell door opened. He winced in the new flood of light but adjusted quickly. Gardina dropped the keys on the floor and dusted off her hands. "The sheriff?" he asked.

Her smile was cool. "He retired early."

He let that go. He didn't at all feel guilty about Jin meeting the Evermore sooner rather than later. He merely stayed close and kept a hand over his gun as he followed Gardina swiftly toward the exit. They encountered no one along the way, thankfully. They slipped out the back of the building and Gardina whistled softly.

A horse grazing not far away lifted its head and then walked over. It sniffed at her curiously before butting against her contentedly. She wasted no time in grabbing a bridle and fastening it on. "Hurry!" she ordered Matthias.

He swung up onto the horse's back and then reached down and tugged her up in front of him. She held on tight as he sent the horse galloping toward the exit of town. They needed to find that safe spot, and soon. He just couldn't shake the feeling that they were still missing something in this scenario. He wanted to be as strong as possible before things went on too much longer. At this point, sanctuary might not do him or Kae any good. He might need to confront Feran directly.

Wouldn't *that* just be a handful of fun?

Chapter Eight

The goblet sailed across the room to crash into the doors of the throne room. Darren had good reflexes, thankfully. The gold and crystal container had missed his head, though the contents had splashed over his shoulders. The red wine made a spreading stain on the floor that he studied dispassionately. It wasn't the first time the floor had been turned red.

Feran was nearly as red and his breath panted out hard. He had tried to put a bounty on Commander Matthias Logan's head, but *no one* in Rikan wanted to take up the hunt. Soldiers were already expressing their displeasure at following orders from anyone except Logan. The civilians were calling for an end to the war. Somehow, he had gained command of the entire country without lifting a finger. "I should have murdered that bastard when I found him!" he raged.

"Why didn't you?"

"*I want the Sovereign!*" His gnarled fingers bit into the arms of his wrongful throne. "Send word to every bandit, thief, and hunter on this forsaken continent! I will offer a king's ransom for Logan to be delivered to me alive!"

"And the Gray Etyrnal?" Darren lifted a brow. "As I said when I arrived, she is by far more deadly than any other Etyrnal I've heard of. In fact, I'd consider her the deadliest creature on the world. Light and Dark themselves seem to have blessed her."

"She is a woman, not a ghost!" Feran spat. "She still lives! All Etyrnals have a weakness, and surely she has one as well! Find it out, use it, and turn her into a weapon against Logan!" Sensing the next question, he countered icily, "Her Runic is useless to me, General Richards. It will respond only to the Campbell bloodline. The Water Runic will only respond to the Vargas bloodline."

And surely the Sovereign would respond only to the Sovereign bloodline. The family had even changed its name to match its Runic. Feran was a distant relative, and no more. It was possible the Sovereign would respond to him, but not likely. He would need to fuse it to a rightful heir and kill off the heir *while* he or she was wearing it in order to change its ownership.

Darren turned on his heel and headed for the door. For a man so dead set on being an Etyrnal, he thought sardonically, Feran knew shit about them. That lack of knowledge was going to be the literal death of him.

    Hopefully sooner rather than later.

Chapter Nine

It was nearly dawn before Gardina and Matthias reached the next town on the road. It was called Lal, and it was bigger than Truan by double. Both were exhausted from the hard ride. Rather than try to go any further, they sought out the biggest inn possible. He registered them as a married couple under a fake name and indicated they were both Etyrnals. The innkeeper was more than happy to take them to one of the special rooms they kept just for the occasional Etyrnal visitor. The windows were covered with double-thick blinds and curtains.

Gardina sealed the door and the windows with her Runic for good measure and then blinked when Matthias suddenly picked her up off her feet. "Matt?"

"Not tonight," he told her softly. "Did you know you're swaying on your feet? You haven't had decent sleep in a few days now, and despite your protests otherwise, you're alive enough to need some rest. We'll get some decent sleep today and set out again tonight. You said you knew a secret place no one could find us."

"Uh-huh." She didn't protest when he put her

down on the bed and turned out the lights. As the welcoming darkness enveloped her, she was suddenly too tired to keep her eyes open. She was asleep long before he tugged off her shoes and tucked her under the covers. She didn't even stir when he joined her and tugged her into his arms safely.

They slept away most of the day. He woke before she did and ordered room service with some of the money she had given him. She started stirring not long after, and he leaned over her where she would see him when she woke. "Good morning," he told her solemnly. "Or evening, as it were. Nice dreams?"

"I don't dream." She sat up with a yawn and a stretch. "Never have, even before getting my Runic. Not normal dreams anyway. I sometimes have lucid ones. More like visions than dreams." She skimmed her hands up over his face and smiled. His hair was damp. "I think Kae isn't the only one who dislikes being dirty."

"After going months without bathing at all, I'm making up for lost time." He eased in for a lingering kiss and slowly smiled. "How is it you never have morning breath?"

"It's a gift." She eyed his neck wistfully, then sighed. Not yet, damn it. Once they were safe in her hidden home, she could indulge her need for him. "I'll be back shortly." She dissolved like morning mist and slipped through his fingers.

Room service had arrived by the time she returned from her hunt. She nibbled on a pastry while he made his way through an entire meal, but she couldn't help noticing that his intake of food had dramatically gone down. Another preparation point. His body was definitely revving him up to become an Etyrnal. He might make the transition easier than anyone else she had known.

She sat down next to him at the table and sighed. "Let's talk about the Sovereign. We have some time before we need to hit the road."

"I swear I don't know anything about it." He pressed his fingers to his eyes. "I mean, I don't know if I know. I was not yet four years old when the coup occurred. I don't really remember my early life at all. Yeah, I know there should be *something* because Human memory can go back to two years of age, but I've got a blank spot. Like you said, and like Jin implied, I probably blocked it from trauma."

She crossed her arms and frowned. "The thing that has me most puzzled is that the Sovereign would be relatively useless to Feran. It can only be used by the royal bloodline. I remember back when I was briefly engaged to Leonasis Sovereign how he joked about there never being worries of sneaking a changeling into the royal family since just bringing the Runic near kids would prove if they had the blood."

He snorted. "I'm sure some parts of the family had wished otherwise."

Somehow she kept her jaw from dropping. She straightened up and looked at him a second time, and this time she began to look closer. There was a red hue to his pupils. Pupils only changed color if the owner had been heavily influenced by a Runic. All Campbells had a gray hue to their pupils, including her. The Sovereign Runic was *red*. He had nearly quoted verbatim Alexander Sovereign's retort to his little brother. He had the rich green eyes of the bloodline.

She almost couldn't breathe as she stared at him. At thirty-four, he was the right age. Was it possible that the bodies of the prince and princess that had been found had been *decoys*? It would explain why Feran had been watching him, and why he was dead certain only he could locate the Sovereign.

"Ghosty?" He gently smoothed her hair out of her face. "You look afraid."

"Threats to the man I love do that," she managed to say, and her voice was relatively normal. No wonder. No wonder she had been drawn to Alexander. Somehow she had known that his descendant was her perfect match. Did that make all of this . . . *destiny*? That was impossible, right? *There were no gods, and there was no Evermore!*

"Well, what do we do next?" he asked.

She huffed out a breath. "You know what? I'm at the point where I say we go to Rikan castle, knock on Feran's door, and ask him and Richards what the hell they want. Make it clear that you don't know anything, and don't have any interest, and that we're happy to stay in Coronia while Feran does whatever he wants."

"You think we can end this without a fight?"

Her brows came together. "Well, yeah. Why not?"

He shook his head. "I want your optimism. I really do." He got to his feet and tugged her up as well. "Alright. We'll try this your way. If we can't talk it out, at least we'll be close enough to remove Feran and Richards as needed. Maybe we can make an *actual* democracy, unlike you Campbells who don't know the definition."

She briefly stuck her tongue out at him, but she was smiling. They cleaned up their room, paid for it, and headed out of the inn. Evening was turning into dusk and lamps were being lit. They were halfway to where their horse was stabled when both sensed danger. A sharp glance around told them that shadowy figures were gathering in the alleys. Word was spreading quickly about the price on Matthias' head.

Gray light rippled over Gardina's Runic mark and fog rolled in out of nowhere. The thick, gray mass obscured vision nearly wholly. She grabbed Matthias' hand and hurried him toward the stable. Much to their surprise, someone had already saddled and released their horse. They only had to swing up onto his back and ride quickly toward a city exit. Only when they were out did the fog lift.

A chill roughened Gardina's skin. Feran had to know Matthias' real identity. He was going to too much trouble for a mere suspicion. She *definitely* needed to transform Matthias. He could probably take Feran on alone without problems, but she didn't trust Richards. He was unusually powerful. Frankly? She kind of suspected he might have Fae blood, too.

Her secret hiding spot was an underground cabin. It was another royal retreat designed to be used when someone *really* didn't want to be found. She took care of opening the hidden door and going inside to light the lamps while Matthias turned their horse loose into the woods. They could retrieve him later; best he not linger and give them away. At that point, Gardina trusted nothing.

She had stirred up the fireplace for heat and light when the area went silvery around her. Her ethereal companion stepped up beside her, and she straightened with a smile. The smile slowly faded as she saw the look on the other woman's face. Something clenched in her heart. "What don't I know?" she whispered.

The silver eyes watching her were saddened. "Gardina, you cannot transform Matthias."

Her fingers clenched together. "As in I literally can't, or I shouldn't?"

"You literally cannot. You are not a normal Etyrnal, little ghost. You are more alive than you think, but you are also still more dead than anything else that lives. You have one foot fully in life and the other fully in death. I will make it simple: to remove a

Greater Runic from any other being will merely make them a normal Etyrnal. To remove yours would be to kill you entirely."

Pain slowly rose and choked her. "How funny," she managed to whisper. "The one thing I want is the one thing I can't have. I'm beginning to almost wish there was actually destiny. That this could be made miraculously right."

Tender fingers skimmed down her hair. "Did I say he would never be an Etyrnal? His future lies down a different path. Did you think he would not find the Sovereign? It calls out for him. Whether you were here or not, he would inevitably find it. Your presence ensures he will survive finding it."

Gardina clenched her hands into fists. "Then why is he my Devoted at all?" she demanded fiercely.

"How else would you have met?" She shrugged lightly. "I had to be sure that you were happy."

For the second time, Gardina almost stopped breathing. "*You* had to be sure? *You* made Matthias my Devoted? But that means you would have to be . . . to be . . ."

Her companion merely smiled and disappeared into her silvery-green color, and the light went back to normal. Yet nothing was normal at all. Gardina's world had gone through its second upheaval in her life. First, to think there was no Evermore and no gods. Now to think that . . . that maybe there *was*. If that *was* the Goddess of Light, then . . . what did she want? What interest did she have in the outcome of these events?

Matthias came down the stairs and shut the door behind him. "We're safe," he started to say. He saw the look on her face and swiftly crossed to pull her into his arms. "What's wrong?" he demanded.

She closed her eyes. "I can't transform you, Matt. I want to. I want to give you eternity. But . . . I am not enough alive." Tears welled and began to slide down her pale skin. "I'm half dead. I can't transform anyone, not even my Devoted. I had another lucid dream. It told me that—that I can't even remove my Runic without dying. I had always suspected so, but having it spelled out . . ."

"Fine."

"Fine?" She looked up sharply and then caught a breath as he gently wiped away her tears. "How can you say that?"

He smiled. "I just don't believe that the gods are that cruel. You can scoff at me, but this time I'm going to believe in a happy ending. And if I'm wrong, then I'll just stay with you until my dying day. I think you've taught me how to be optimistic, Ghosty. Maybe I can teach you to believe again."

Too late for that. She was definitely back on the road toward being a believer. It was just as painful as learning to not believe. She put it aside and drew a deep breath. "I guess there's a bright side to this," she admitted softly. She found herself smiling. "I can bite you all I like without any problems." She eased up and teasingly nipped at his neck. "I didn't feed that well earlier," she warned huskily. "I'm . . . hungry."

"You're not the only one." He buried his fingers in her hair and dragged her up for the kisses he craved more than air. Her incisors had lengthened again and he teased them lightly with his tongue. She retaliated by nipping at his lower lip just hard enough to sting.

She gave a breathless giggle as he scooped her off her feet and whirled to drop her onto the bed. She bounced twice on the plush mattress and shot an impish grin at him. "Don't jump on here with me. I'd go through the roof."

He stared at her for a moment and wondered how it was even possible she could be half-dead at all.

She burned with life. The flush to her face and the light in her golden eyes made her more radiantly alive than any other creature in existence. Perhaps that was the Light inside the Gray of her soul. The Dark was what allowed her to endure trials and willingly send on the ones who had lost their way. He could easily believe that the gods loved her most. In a way . . . she was their daughter.

She rolled up to her knees and started unlacing his tunic. Her fingers delicately skimmed over his skin as she revealed it, and her lips teased his. "Don't forget to take off your boots first," she warned huskily. "I can't imagine how awkward it might be to attempt to get your pants off and trip yourself flat."

"If I trip, I'll aim to land on the bed." He stripped off the tunic and then returned the favor by helping her get hers off as well. He did remove his boots first, and they ended up in the pile with her shoes as well. Hands tugged and teased until they were both naked.

His eyes devoured her eagerly. Not that he had much by way of comparison, but he found her to be perfect for him. If the Runic had missed letting her reach some sort of peak of maturity, it had not missed it by much. There was no mistaking her for a girl. She was every inch a woman.

Her contented sigh echoed his. She had a comparison, and he still by far won. His soldier's body had been honed by war and battle. Hard muscle and strong skin flecked by small scars. And some not so small scars. Her fingers trembled as she lightly touched what looked like a particularly nasty gouge across his ribs. "Matt."

"I don't remember it. It's from that time. It's in the past." He dragged her up for a nearly ravenous kiss and tumbled her over onto the bed. He caught his weight on his elbows to keep them from bouncing too much, but they did still jostle a bit. "What's with you royals and your fluffy beds?" he muttered as he nipped at her neck in teasing retaliation.

"It's not the fluff. It's the springs. And if you've never jumped on a bed before, you've missed more than I thought. We can remedy that later." She moaned softly as his questing lips tormented the sensitive skin of her breasts. Her skin had always been very tender around her Runic mark, and it seemed even more so now. Something about him just made *everything* more than it had been. He made her entire world more wonderful.

His   desire   to

explore and caress every inch of her body made his lack of experience moot. He didn't wholly know where he was going or what he was doing, and she didn't mind at all. He was driving her crazy, but she didn't care. When his lips captured one taut nipple, the jolt of sheer pleasure made her arch against him. A potent blend of hungers churned inside her body.

She twisted her body sharply and he fell over onto the bed with a teasing laugh. "I forget how strong you are." He caught a handful of her hair and tugged her down for a greedy kiss. He couldn't seem to get enough of her taste. It gave him a whole new respect for her hunger for him.

She eagerly petted and caressed his body the way he had done to her, and the feel of him quivering beneath her was empowering. Her heightened senses took delight in everything. His scent and taste and feel. The way his darkened eyes watched her as if she was a goddess herself. His pulse throbbed and beckoned in his neck temptingly.

He sat up to grab for her, and a groan rumbled in his chest as her mouth fastened hotly to his skin. Her teeth scraped and bit in, and it again sent that shocking blast of erotic delight through his nerves. Unable to wait another moment without having her, he adjusted their position slightly and then began to press his throbbing arousal deep into her waiting warmth. Her moan vibrated through his neck as she bit deeper in response.

She drank deep as he drove into her again and again, and the glow that began to effuse her body was beautiful and arousing. Eventually, neither of them could bear any more and ecstasy tore through them both in wicked waves. Somehow, he managed to bury himself deeper, and her teeth pierced just that little bit extra. Only his groan vibrated on the air. Hers was muffled by his neck. They collapsed into a sweaty and exhausted heap and fought to find a steady breath.

The feel of her delicately licking the bite mark made him say roughly, "Did you just lick me?"

She stirred only enough to drape herself more thoroughly over him. She had no desire to move anywhere. She had *never* felt that happy before in her life. In fact, she didn't think she had ever fed that well, either. "After how long I had my teeth in you," she countered drowsily, "you're surprised by a lick?"

"I suppose that's fair." He caught an edge of the blankets with his fingers and then tugged them up and over them both. He sighed long and deep and curled his arms around her waist. He had never felt happier in his life. "I still think I'll get a chance to return the favor eventually. I wonder what I'll be."

The Sovereign was a Dark Runic. Rather than say that, she said instead, "You should be Dark. It suits you more than Light. You're not optimistic enough yet. Maybe it's a good reason you're not going to be Gray like me." She tilted her head back and gave him the impish smile he loved. "I'm not sure I'd know what to do with you if you started believing in the greater good."

"Laugh at me more, probably. Which I don't mind." He stretched long and tucked his hands under his head. "Strange that it would take an absolute upheaval of my life for me to feel this peaceful, but I'm not complaining. Are you happy?"

"You have to ask?" She rubbed her cheek slowly over his skin. "Would I be happier if you were now an Etyrnal? Yes. Am I happy just to be with you anyway? *Hell* yes."

"The extreme bite should have transformed me? I admit, it felt different from when you first bit me."

"I bit deep enough that my saliva got into you," she concurred. "Which, yes, should have started the transformation. The fact that I didn't have any control over the depth of my bite tells me that we should be glad that you had decided you *wanted* to be transformed. We never did learn that rain dance."

It made him laugh, of course. He shifted his gaze around the cabin and found that it looked no different from any other cabin except for its lack of windows. "Runic Master of the Soil variety?" he asked curiously.

"Right." She reluctantly got off his chest and slipped out of bed. "Fire's magic, too. Let me put the hearth cover on it. We'll get the heat without the light so we can sleep." She knelt down, and he knelt beside her. Her breath caught as he drew her up into his arms and hotly pressed a kiss to her shoulder. "Matt."

"We can rest later. The night is only beginning." He slowly lowered her to the rug and admired the way her white hair spilled around her in untamed curls. More than ever, she felt familiar to him. In a way, he didn't care anymore what the past held. His future lay in the beautiful gold eyes watching him. Come hell or high water, he would find a way to claim eternity. They would *not* be cheated out of it.

They woke up in the morning to find themselves tangled together in the blankets. Neither minded. They rousted enough food for Matthias to eat—though his intake was still low—and Gardina nibbled on another pastry. She had a sweet tooth that he found endearing. Once they were both fueled, they returned the cabin to proper order and set out into the woods to find their wandering horse. No more towns for them. They wouldn't stop until they were in the Coronia capitol known as Stonia.

Little over a week later, they were finally in the massive port city. It spanned the tops and bottoms of the cliffs alike, and the palace rose over it like a shimmering jewel. It had been a week of nearly nonstop travel, but it had been worth it. They both felt better once they were within the confines of the large city. It would be damned stupid to attack them in the middle of the capitol of the country that *still* saw Gardina as its princess.

The first thing to do was to petition for sanctuary. Gardina took care of that while Matthias saw about getting them passage on the next ship heading for Rikan. It was an odd thing to ask for sanctuary and then to plan to leave, but they couldn't hide in Stonia forever. There was still Kae to be concerned about; Feran had shown interest in her as well.

The next ship was not sailing until the following morning. That suited Matthias fine. As evening came, he went looking for his lover. He could just faintly hear the sound of her flute calling, and it slowly drew him around the outskirts of the castle itself and toward the cliffs that looked down onto the restless ocean below. He found her standing at the edge and playing a melancholy piece that cried as softly as the sea breezes whipping her hair and skirts around her body.

He moved closer and slid his arms around her waist. She lowered the flute and said nothing as she stood in the circle of his embrace. Finally, softly, she said, "I died here."

He took a long breath and held her closer. "Tell me."

"When I was twenty," she began softly, "I was engaged to marry Leonasis Sovereign from the Rikan kingdom. He was the youngest of three brothers. I would have preferred his elder brother, but he was madly in love with his fiancée." She smiled. "They were so cute together."

"Did you at least like Leonasis?"

"Like, yes. Felt mild attraction, yes. Love and

desire the way I feel for you? Not *even* close." She sighed. "There just weren't any sparks between us. He just didn't smell right, somehow. I decided to surprise him at his cottage and see if we could strike up aforementioned sparks."

He grimaced. "Uh-oh."

"Caught him with his pants down," she confirmed with characteristic cheer. "I've grown to find that part kind of funny over the years. Especially remembering how my father bellowed 'fetch him and make sure his pants are on!' when he found out." She sighed. "His smell? Yeah, he smelled like women's perfume. He had been cheating on me so often and so vagrantly that he had absorbed the scent. Thank the moons I had decided to play the proper princess and wait until marriage. I expected nothing but fidelity from him, and I didn't even get that."

"So he was an idiot." He rested his chin on her shoulder. "How did that lead to you finding the Runic?" He refused to call it her death. She was half-alive, and that was more than enough for him.

"I went for a walk that night." She had never even told Selene and Niall the gory details, but she wanted Matthias to know everything. He had given her the strength to look back. "I came here and was watching the ocean." She closed her eyes. "Seems Leo lost it. Refused to go home disgraced. He came after me with a sword. It's almost funny, actually. He didn't even touch me. I lost my balance and fell over the side." Her eyes opened slightly. "The impact with the ocean broke every bone in my body. I was dead even before I sank beneath the waves. My hand touched the Ghost Runic and it ripped me back. Hurt like nothing I've ever felt."

"That's when you stopped believing?

"Well, yes. I died. I saw nothing on the other side. There was nothing but blackness. No Evermore."

"Gardina . . . are you *sure* you saw the other side?"

She turned and frowned. "I died. Of course I did."

"But *did* you?" he persisted. "You were cognizant until you found the Runic, right? If you were cognizant during death, then you can't say you saw the other side. That blackness? Sounds like you went *unconscious*. Didn't you tell me that transformation under traumatic circumstances can force longer rest?"

Her mouth opened, then closed. A tremor began to run through her body. Even if she hadn't already been shaken by Light's presence, this would have made her doubt anew. She dropped her head onto his chest and fought the shivers rippling through her skin. His arms closed around her tighter and his warmth seeped inside to her soul. "I don't know what to believe anymore," she whispered.

"You don't have to believe in anything except the fact that I love you and I will always be here to remind

you that you are still half-alive."

She drew a deep breath and eased back. "Matt." She reached up to frame his face tenderly. "If you do not become an Etyrnal someday, then I will remove my Runic after you take your last breath. I will go with you into whatever may lay beyond death, whether it is some mystical realm or simply nothing at all."

It humbled him. Needing to bring back her smile, he lifted her off her feet and strode away from the site of her rebirth. He would never see it as the site of her death. "If you're going to get romantic and mushy on me, we're going back to the inn and you're going to teach me how to jump on beds."

She started giggling. "While I'm in it with you?"

He   shot   her   a   wicked   grin.   "Eventually."

Chapter Ten

Selene and Niall kept a cabin on the outskirts of the city known as Grian. It was many days from Truan and it was much bigger. It had taken a little less than a week to reach home, thanks to needing to travel with Kae. The two Etyrnals normally flew and made the journey quicker. Not that they had minded the longer trip. Kae was a delight.

She asked a million questions, showed excitement for every new sight or experience, and she was relatively well-behaved for her age. She had even convinced the two Etyrnals to let her keep a wild grumbler—a wild feline—that she had since named Snacks since it liked them so much. Niall was tickled at the idea of giving Matthias his daughter back and handing over the pet at the same time.

The first few days in the cabin were perfectly normal and peaceful. Not a lick of danger even tried to approach the cabin. It was just as well. On the morning of the third day, Kae came downstairs with a new set of problems. She walked into the kitchen and complained, "I can't sleep. I hurt."

Selene immediately moved to her side and

knelt down. "What hurts, little one? Is it an old pain? I told you that some may come back over the years until you recovered fully from the trauma."

"It's different." She rubbed at her eyes and tried to hide her sniffles. Her other hand clutched the stuffed toy that Niall had bought her. "My back hurts and it itches." She held out her arms and cuddled close as Selene picked her up.

Selene carried her back to her room and gently put her down on her stomach on the bed. She tugged up the nightgown the girl wore and immediately saw the problem. Her skin had turned a familiar, furious red color and the muscles were visibly bunched and knotted. Bruising was beginning to form as well. "Huh-oh. Stay here, baby. Let me go get some herbs for you to eat."

Niall was waiting for her in the kitchen and he lifted a brow as he saw her digging in cabinets. "What's wrong with our little lady?"

"The half of her that is Fae is overriding the half that is Human. She's growing in her wings. We're going to need Kane to come help. He's the only person I know with the hands steady enough to open the skin of her back without damaging her newborn wings."

He winced. "That

don't sound like a pleasant prospect. It's a wonder that Fae even want their wings after that."

"It's only because she is half-Fae." She took down the herbs she needed and began mixing a pain reliever. "If she was whole, she would have been born with them in place. We could let the process go on as it is, but she will be in a great deal of agony and there is no knowing if she might not do permanent damage to herself."

He sighed. "I'll write to Kane. I reckon he'll be glad for the vacation."

Vladimir Kane, just Kane to all who knew him, was a distant cousin to the Campbell royal house and a hunter within his own right. Rather than hunt ghosts, he was a hunter of the *nosferatu*: Etyrnals who had gone mad on their power and sought only to bathe in the blood of others. It happened infrequently, but still often enough that an Etyrnal Hunter like Kane was needed. His unwavering calm and steel nerves had, perhaps unsurprisingly, made him into an ideal surgeon's assistant as well.

There were many mysteries to Kane, and there were things Niall still didn't know, though he had his guesses. Neither Gardina nor Selene were forthcoming, and he was fine with that. If he had noticed certain characteristics inside Kane that had been inside himself—and Matthias—he kept his mouth shut. It wasn't his business.

While Selene gave Kae her medication and set about making breakfast, he wrote a quick letter and headed outside to mail it. A bird with a missive was already sitting on the box, and he freed the letter from the avian pouch. The handwriting made him snort. "And Ghosty says there's no fate." He carried the note inside and called, "Kane wrote to us."

Selene arched a brow. "That does not bode well." She took the letter and opened it. She winced within the first few lines. "He's in Ashfort. He's been grounded."

Grounding a hunter meant that said hunter had been badly wounded. Niall winced as well. "How bad?"

"Badly enough that he's requesting my immediate aid. The *nosferatu* he has been pursuing got to him first." She tucked the note away and sighed. "Well, I suppose we shall take care of two problems at once. I will put him back together and he can help me with Kae." Under her breath, she added, "I would never let you do this sort of thing. What is Riki thinking?"

"Riki?" Niall asked politely.

She didn't answer. "Kae!" she called up the stairs. "Pack your bags, little one. We're going to visit Gardina's cousin."

"Okay!"

Niall blocked the doorway before Selene could go past. "Selene." It was said with infinite patience. "I have not pressed for answers, but if I can help, y'know I damned well will. Is Kane a Devoted?"

"Yes."

"Does he know?"

"No."

"Was he injured by *that* Light Etyrnal?"

"I do not know," she sighed. She let her head rest briefly on his shoulder. "My instincts say he was. He is getting close, Niall. I do not know what his life will be like when he succeeds. It scares me."

"Alright." He kissed her gently. "He's strong, love. He's much like his cousin, despite their protests to the contrary. He'll be fine. Let's go pay him a visit."

Traveling during the day would be ideal since it would get them to Ashfort at night and Selene's power would be useable. It was why she had been forced to resort to old-fashioned medications to help

Kae's back pain.

Once they had packed up their bags, they used the four-foot grumbler as a reluctant pack-mule. The feline grumbled more but didn't truly protest since Kae hugged him and promised him treats later. It was only until Grian anyway. They would catch a carriage from the city to Ashfort.

Kae didn't mind going on another trip. She thought that Ghosty's cousin was probably going to be really nice since Ghosty had said she loved him. Truthfully, nothing about the entire situation had thrown Kae off-stride. She usually got answers to her questions before she had to ask them. The only thing that she didn't know was the identity of the pretty man occasionally following them. Neither Selene nor Niall had seen him, and he looked really translucent, so maybe he was in her imagination.

As far as imaginary friends went, he was nice. He had a very handsome face that she liked to look at, and he had kind eyes. He was often grumpy and seemed to have a temper, but he smiled at her if he found her watching him. He had wings, too. She liked them. She felt really safe with him, though she just felt like he wanted her to do something. If he would just *tell* her, then maybe she could help. Adults were so silly.

She rested her head on Niall's shoulder as he carried her, and she contemplated the things that had happened. Her mommy and daddy were fighting a bad guy. They hadn't come back for her yet. That probably meant they needed help. She looked to where her imaginary friend stood and wondered if he could help.

He glanced at her with a lifted brow as if he could read her mind and then he sighed and disappeared. It made her feel better. He could help. But, seriously, if there were going to be any more fights against bad guys, she was going to help, too.

Chapter Eleven

"So they're on their way here?" Feran's eyes narrowed on Darren. "That had better not be a joke."

Though slightly more wan than he had last looked, Darren inclined his head with all of his normal grace. "It is no joke. They petitioned for sanctuary and then bought tickets for a ship out this direction. Logan must have remembered where the Sovereign is kept."

"That saves us the trouble of trying to get them in Stonia." Feran broke off for a coughing fit that stained his fingers with blood by the end. "Send out a ship to intercept them! Bring them here directly. At your recommendation, I sent for the Fae artifact that might render the Gray Etyrnal helpless. She will be a valuable tool against Logan."

Darren inclined his head and turned to leave the room. He had to walk carefully. His entire body had begun to feel as if it wasn't under his control anymore. He would find himself going places and doing things he was not conscious of telling himself to do. It almost felt as if something was fighting for possession of his body.

How ironic would it be that he might have to ask for help with an exorcism from the Ghost Hunter he had tried to kill? Perhaps he could barter Logan's life for his own. The bonds of a Devoted could be powerful.

Chapter Twelve

The first two days out at sea for Gardina and Matthias were peaceful. They had crossed over into Rikan territory and there was no telling when the peace might change, though. They did their best to enjoy the sail regardless of the danger, and Gardina discovered a new side in her lover. Someone had never been on a ship before.

He ran around like a boy, asking a million questions and poking his nose into all of the workings. Something told her that their future house might have to be on the water so that he could sail all he wanted. That suited her fine. She had loved her manor in the woods, but she loved the ocean equally. Maybe they could rebuild her manor along the shore. Perhaps between the two countries. It would be symbolically apt. She knew Kae would love it.

"Ah ha." Matthias slid his arms around her waist and tugged her close so they could share the view over the side. "I could nearly hear you thinking. What has you smiling?"

"You." She snuggled close. "Finish pestering the captain?

A hint of a sheepish smile crossed his face. "For

now. No wonder I'm amusing you." He nuzzled her ear. "I can't help it. There are a lot of things I've never gotten to do. You've given me a chance to do them. If you're the innocence lost to adults, I'm glad I found you." Softer, he added, "And thank you, for sharing what happened to you. I can see why you hesitated. I'm not sure I'd have been able to handle it before. It still scares me. And, strangely, offends me. What happened to your fiancé anyway?"

She covered his hands with hers and smiled wryly. "It was a sketchy thing. They couldn't hang him for murder because I was still technically alive. On the other hand, I was also technically dead, and if I hadn't found the Runic, I'd be *all* dead. My kingdom wanted him hanged anyway. His elder brother decided that Leo might as well endure a half-life of his own. My parents concurred."

"And . . .?"

"He lived the rest of his life as a eunuch."

"How fitting."

"I thought so. He actually didn't live very long anyway. He got quite sickly after he tried to kill me. It was as if his lifeforce leeched away. He died by age forty."

"Pardon my saying so, but that sounds like he pissed off the patrons of the Etyrnal race."

"I don't mind you saying it, and I'm beginning to suspect you're right. All the things I've written off as coincidence don't feel so coincidental anymore." She sighed. "Will you call me insane if I tell you that my aforementioned lucid dreams involved talking to whom I thought was my Runic spirit, but might in fact have been the Goddess of Light herself?"

"I won't call you insane. I'll just say 'I told you so' and let it be." He nipped at her ear softly and enjoyed the sound of her breath breaking. "Let's enjoy the half-alive part of your existence," he murmured huskily.

She was being distracted but she didn't mind at all. She turned in his arms and feathered her lips across his. "I find I have the munchies," she told him solemnly, a tone marred by the laughter lurking inside. The laughter became giggles as he promptly lifted her off her feet and began striding toward their cabin. Walking was overrated anyway.

The captain and crew alike watched them with smiles. They had known Gardina for years since they operated mainly out of Stonia. They normally carried just cargo, but once they had heard that she was assisting the refugee from Rikan, they had volunteered their services. Seeing her happier and more content than they ever had before, they sent up thanks to Light and Dark equally.

The happiness did not last much longer. As afternoon was creeping into evening, an odd whistling noise made Matthias look up with a frown from where Gardina had been trying to teach him how to fish. The whistle was strangely familiar, and he froze when he realized why. "Get down!" he ordered sharply as he hit the deck with Gardina in his arms.

He had an impressive ability to compel obedience, and everyone dropped flat. A flaming cannonball smashed into the mast moments later and cracked it in half. Sailors had to hastily scramble out of the way of the debris, and others rushed to put out the fire. Gardina shoved out of Matthias' grip and hurried over to the captain. He handed her the spyglass without a word.

Her stomach sank as she saw what approached. Four ships bearing the colors of Rikan. They were preparing more shots. The first had been merely a warning. She looked again, and she spotted the familiar figure of Darren Richards on one of the ships. "They know you're here," she told Matthias. She handed the glass back to the captain. "We intended to encounter Richards all along, but on *our* terms. We need to even the ground."

Gray power whipped around her body as her Runic began to glow. The ocean began to seethe restlessly and a whirlpool opened. From deep within the depths of the vortex rose an immense wreckage of a ship. It was still relatively intact though deeply damaged and decayed, and ghostly sails began to drop from the masts. The undead crew began to load and fire cannons, and the impact of the ammo was no figment. It blew out a massive hole in the first enemy ship.

Matthias had taken command on the freighter ship; a battle was a battle whether it was on the sea or not, and the captain willingly deferred to his greater experience. The ghost ship was a good decoy and kept three enemies busy, but Darren managed to navigate his through the mess and open fire on the freighter again.

The cargo ship had never been intended to endure that sort of abuse. It began to crack apart with every consecutive strike. A particularly potent blast of fire magic and gunpowder devastated the back end of the freighter. The impact was violent enough to send several people overboard, and Matthias was one of them. He hit hard, and he sank almost immediately beneath the surface.

He didn't come back up, and Gardina went as white as her clothes. He had never been on a ship. He had never lived anywhere but the relatively waterless Rikan. *He didn't know how to swim!* She scrambled for the side and dove into the ocean. She would be damned if the sea took anything else from her, and as soon as everything was done, she was throwing him in a lake with Kae and teaching them both!

Matthias tried to struggle back toward the surface, but he didn't seem to be going anywhere. His lungs were burning, *starving*, for air. A violent curse echoed internally as he realized that life was even more bitterly unfair than he had thought. Was he going to die there? No answers, no hope. No chance to share eternity with his beautiful ghost. He would *not* accept that!

Almost as soon as he had the thought, and almost as soon as he felt the fierce will to *live*, he felt something else entirely. It was hot and powerful and welled inside his body so strongly that he would have gagged if he hadn't been drowning. An odd reddish glow lit the area around him but he barely noticed it. The last bubble of air slipped from his lips as he started to sink deeper. Something caught him and held him suspended instead.

The glow gave away his location and Gardina swam quickly to him. Her Runic had taken over her lungs as well, and she could hold her breath as long as needed, though it stung. She grabbed her lover and propelled him as fast as she could toward the surface. A strange force helped guide them faster, and they broke through the surface. She sucked in a grateful breath of air and looked around sharply. Chunks of debris surrounded them while the ships continued to duke it out in the distance.

She dragged Matthias to one of the biggest pieces and shoved him onto it. There was no room for her so she hovered beside him instead. He wasn't breathing. She didn't even notice she was crying as she pushed on his chest and fought fiercely to make him take in air. He suddenly convulsed and began coughing up the seawater he had inhaled. She turned him onto his side to help and very nearly lost her lift in relief.

The coughing faded though he didn't wake, but at least he was alive. She buried her face in her hands on a broken sound. And she had thought that losing him to old age would be hard. Losing him before his time would have destroyed her. Hearing his voice crying out to her that he did not want to leave would haunt her for the rest of time.

She looked back toward the restless waves and frowned. She would have *sworn* she had seen, well, someone holding him from sinking deeper. The red glow had her confused as well. She turned him onto his back again to look for the source, and she found it literally embedded in his lower arm. Emerging from the trace remains of his family mark was a glowing red Runic. Shock took her voice and her breath alike.

She carefully touched it, and it immediately came free and bounced onto the wood planking. She gingerly picked it up and found herself looking at a familiar symbol inside the small globe. The symbol of Sovereign. The Runic pulsed and burned with so much power that it could be nothing less than the Greater Sovereign Runic itself. It had been hidden inside Matthias' body all along.

It was not impossible. Runics, both Greater and Lesser, could be housed inside the flesh of the living even without being fused. It was effectively useless to the holder, though. A housed Runic did not impart anything at all. No magic, no nothing. Greaters would not make the bearer an Etyrnal. It *would* enhance natural gifts, but no more. Perhaps it had been the Sovereign all along that had been preparing Matthias for transformation. It had enhanced his natural Devoted gifts.

Somehow, during the coup, someone had hidden the Runic inside him for safety. The body of the prince that had been found? She was beginning to suspect that perhaps *that* had been the real Matthias Logan. She hesitated for a moment and then drew out her logbook from her Runic. She furled pages until the entries went back thirty years, and she slowed as she looked for the night of the massacre. She had never bothered to look before, and now the answer jumped out.

Tobias Sovereign: Unconfirmed

After a brief hesitation, she drew her finger across where *Unconfirmed* was written and it immediately changed to *Alive*. The entry disappeared entirely; the book only recorded those whose ghosts had not been found. She sent the book away and looked to the side. The enemy ships were approaching quickly. She only had a few moments to choose.

The only safe place to carry the Sovereign was

within her own Ghost Runic. Being Gray, it could carry Runics of either orientation. She would have to sacrifice something she was already carrying, and that meant either her matches or her flute had to go. The matches were too practical to give up. She removed the flute and dropped it into the ocean. The Sovereign Runic took its place, and hidden inside the Ghost, it would never be detectable. It hurt to watch her flute float away but she could always get another one. She really needed to stop forming attachments to physical things. Maybe it was another of her 'innocent' quirks.

The enemy ships slowed as they drew close, and she felt savage satisfaction that they weren't intact. She looked up at where Darren was staring down at her, and she asked calmly, "Where is the freighter?"

"We sent them on their way. We're only interested in you." He arched a brow at her. "Are you going to make this easy, or should we just go kill the freighter crew anyway?"

"As a matter of fact," she retorted with royal dignity, "we were coming to see you and your king anyway. People escape war frequently enough and go to neutral lands for sanctuary. Yeah, Matt is high ranked for that, but it happens. The pursuit to get him back? A bit much. You having that much trouble being in charge, General Richards?"

"I always forget how smart-mouthed Etyrnals can be," he noted sardonically.

"We're old enough to come up with good comebacks." Her eyes narrowed sharply as a rowboat approached. "You will treat my Devoted with care or you will be dead where you sit. Never forget that I am playing by your rules at my own choice. The gods favor me."

The fact that the sky briefly went dark and the ocean rumbled warningly in the wake of her words was enough to unnerve several soldiers. It kind of unnerved Gardina, too. She had been *bluffing*. She watched intently as they cuffed Matthias and pulled him onto the rowboat, and she went translucent when they reached for her instead. "Not a chance, jerks. I don't need to be bound. As if I'd leave his side!"

No one argued, and they shortly believed she meant what she said. She never left Matthias's side as he was place into one of the brig cells, and it almost seemed as if she had tuned out everyone else in the world entirely. Even Darren felt a bit humbled to see the evidence of her Devotion. An odd sense of regret moved through his heart. Along with his lack of control over his body was coming a lack of control over his emotions. Since when did he care about anything?

Matthias still hadn't awakened by the time they reached Rikan. It didn't surprise Gardina. His entire system had been thrown into a spin between the near drowning and the loss of the Sovereign. His body had been used to the subtle sensation of power. Taking it away without him fusing it promptly had basically put him into withdrawal. She let him sleep, and Darren did as well.

They were both tossed into a dungeon cell while Darren went to report to Feran. The general knelt before his king and dispassionately noticed the deeper gaunt frame and the sickly pallor to his skin. Sanity was slowly being replaced by madness as the sickness ate at his mind as sharply as it ate at his body.

"Well?" Feran barked.

"We have the Etyrnal and Logan alike." Darren kept his gaze lowered. "Logan is unconscious. Nearly drowned, frankly. His Etyrnal saved him. She has yet to flee and has stated she has no intentions of doing so as long as Logan in our hands. She could be convinced to speak with you. If there is anything Logan knows, then she likely knows it as well. I suspect they might be lovers as well."

"Bring her here!" Feran spat. "We have the artifact that will render her powers null. I only have two months left, General Richards! There is no time for niceties!"

Not that he even *knew* what niceties were. Darren merely shrugged and gestured for his men to go retrieve Gardina.

She arrived at the throne room without any problems, and she walked across the porcelain floor with the grace of a princess. She sketched a mocking curtsey to Feran and said, "My parents always taught me to be polite even when confronting a skunk."

Feran stared at her. He had not at all expected her to look as young as she did, and he certainly hadn't expected her to be that utterly lovely. Strangely, he had trouble focusing on her. She seemed to come and go before his eyes. A quick look around had him spotting several soldiers rubbing their eyes. At least he wasn't the only one. "What is your name?" he demanded.

A white brow arched delicately over gold eyes. "Gardina de Coronia of the Campbell Royal Family.

Or, as I am more commonly addressed in the new century, Gardina Campbell. I was almost a queen, but I kind of died."

Several jaws dropped. Feran almost couldn't find his voice or his footing for a moment. "Why do you travel with Commander Logan?" he finally asked.

She sighed. "For the love of the moons, how many times have I got to say this? Matthias is my Devoted. He was born on the only night when the Ghost Moon was full by itself in the sky. I am driven to protect him until his dying day. On top of that, I happen to be in love with him." She shrugged. "I would transform him into an Etyrnal, as Devoted can be, if it weren't for the fact that I'm half-dead."

"You know who he is. You have to know!" Feran aimed a gnarled finger at her. "Where is the Runic?" She tugged aside her tunic and pointed to the mark on her chest, and he spat, "Not *your* Runic! The Sovereign Runic! He must have told you!"

"Sorry, but no. He doesn't know anything about it, and he doesn't remember his childhood before the coup. You want to fill it in? Why are you so fixated on him? He was the son of a servant."

"Once we pry those memories out, you'll find

out for yourself!" He made a gesture.

Her body tensed. "Hate to tell you, but trying to subject him to a second trauma is only going to make me send you to the Evermore sooner rather than later. I hear they have a special place for people like you." She sensed movement but could not get away in time. Something was shoved around her neck and locked into place.

Her power cut off so sharply that she gagged and fell to her knees. She clawed at the necklace as she struggled to take in air. She knew it for what it was: a nullifier. Fae had used them for millennia to help struggling Fae children learn their skills. When placed on an Etyrnal, it completely rendered their power useless. Even at their peak of power, they would be weakened.

Speculation had said that True Etyrnals might risk shattering their Runic. She could believe it. Her Runic was her heart, and it had ceased to beat. She reached for the depths of her strength and cried out to the powers she did not wholly believe in for salvation. She could not say what answered her, but her Runic responded enough to begin beating again. She sucked in air and braced her hands on the ground before she fell over.

A booted foot landed in her side with enough force to send her tumbling across the floor. She landed painfully at Feran's feet, and he leaned down to grab a handful of her hair. "We're thinking that roughing you up a bit might be traumatic enough for him," he taunted her. "He watched his family cut down in front of him. Seeing his precious lover in such painful condition might shake loose those memories."

Cutting off her power in no way made her wholly helpless. Her fingers hooked like claws and she went for his face. Her nails raked open the skin of his cheeks and he jerked back on a howl of pain. His free hand smashed into her jaw and split her lip. She fought off the stars in her head and spit some of her blood in his eye. His howl became a scream as he dropped her onto the ground. A guard hurled her violently aside and she crashed into a set of armor that collapsed on her head. She managed to protect herself with her arms, but bruises were already forming on her fair skin.

Darren was trying to carefully wipe away the gray liquid, but it was too late. One of Feran's eyes had already been blinded. Softly, tauntingly, Gardina said, "Beat me until I'm bloody and you'll only kill yourself. Didn't you know that the blood of an Etyrnal can become a weapon?"

His remaining good eye was feral as it landed on her. He ripped a rifle out of the hands of a soldier and rushed at her. Caught in the mess of armor, she couldn't get away. She ducked and threw her arms over her head protectively. She could not die, but that did not mean she wouldn't get damned close.

Every blow of the rifle butt was agonizing. She bit back every cry or sob that wanted to get free. Her consciousness narrowed to surviving the rain of torture. It all blurred into a single white-hot mess of pain. She didn't even notice when he switched to kicking her. There wasn't an inch left of her body that did not hurt. She could feel the blood staining her skin and knew it had joined the legacy of blood on the floor. Traumatize Matthias? In this state, he might fly into a killing rage.

"Enough!" Darren grabbed Feran and dragged him away from Gardina. Nausea churned his stomach and made his skin even whiter than the downed ghost. He had thought a few slaps, a few hits, maybe even a few bloody marks would be enough. This . . . this was a new level of torture. This had nothing to do with traumatizing Logan. This would have been murder if she had been any other creature.

She lay curled up on the floor in a pool of her

own blood. Ragged breaths were the only sign that she was still at least half-alive. Where she didn't have gouges or split skin, she had bruises. She probably had several broken bones. She had an exceptionally delicate frame to begin with, and Feran wore metal-tipped boots.

The king began to cough and shake, and Darren handed him off to a guard. Disgust lined both their faces equally. "Get him to his chambers, and clean those shoes before you touch them." He pulled gloves out of his pocket and tugged them on. He took the blanket he was offered and knelt to wrap it around Gardina. Her darkened eyes met his defiantly and he knew she was not even dented let alone broken.

He wrapped her carefully and lifted her with surprising gentleness into his arms. He looked at another guard and ordered, "Get water, cloth, bandages, and ointments and then meet me in the dungeon."

Miraculously, Matthias was still unconscious. Darren gingerly placed Gardina on the second cot in the cell and started removing the ruined remains of her clothing. Her eyes opened enough to watch him but she said nothing. When the things he had ordered arrived, he set about cleaning the wounds, dressing them, and binding them. His stomach churned anew as he saw just how much of her body was covered by the white strips of cloth. She almost did not need the new clothing another guard brought.

She remained silent the entire time though her breath caught if he touched something exceptionally tender. Perhaps another miracle, she had no actual broken bones. Possibly a few cracked ribs, but everything else seemed intact. Even without power, an Etyrnal had an exceptionally strong endurance.

As he was leaving, she finally asked softly, "Why?"

He paused but didn't turn around. "I don't know. I'm losing control of my body. My mind. There's something inside me. Can you remove it?"

After a long study of him, she sighed. "No. Whatever is inside you is not a ghost. I'd help you if I could, but I can't. At least that explains your wavery aura. Whatever is inside you is affecting everything about you." Her lashes drooped as exhaustion stole inside. "Your king does not have two months." Her words began to slur. "He has maybe two weeks."

"I had wondered." He glanced back at her. "Logan can remove the necklace when he wakes. I don't have the strength, sorry. And . . . I'm sorry for what happened. It was too much."

"Is that you or the Other speaking?"

"I think . . . it might be both." He shut and locked the door behind himself and then left the dungeon. He flicked off the lights as he went, and the entire area was plunged into darkness.

Grateful for the fact that she would be able to sleep, she gingerly tried to pull the blanket more over her shivering body. She had not lied to him. She could not help him, and what was inside him was not a ghost. She *did* know what it was, though. Maybe there was a better reason for why Darren Richards' name had been in her logbook than merely him faking his death.

Lacking the will to think about it, she closed her eyes and sought her dreamless sleep. She would need all of her strength to hold Matthias together if he truly was traumatized enough to remember his childhood.

Chapter Thirteen

The coach carrying Niall, Selene, and Kae arrived in Ashfort only a few days after setting out. Snacks slept on one of the seats while the Etyrnals sat on the other. Kae was curled up and sleeping on Niall's lap. She had slept for most of the trip, thankfully. Even when Selene's power was at its peak, she could do little to aid Kae's pain. Natural processes of a body simply could not be healed.

The redness on Kae's back had become sores that seeped out blood. Her skin had become as taut as stone. Niall could only liken it to a butterfly sleeping within a cocoon. Frankly, he thought Kae would be better off if she *had* a cocoon. Poor mite was miserable.

The carriage dropped them off right outside the cottage where Kane lived when he wasn't on the hunt. The front was surrounded by lush flowers always in bloom, and the weathered wood of the building itself had aged well.

Kae began to stir as Niall pounded on the front door, and her eyes opened slightly. She didn't know what to expect from Gardina's cousin, but she fell far short of her suspicions when she got her first sight of Vladimir Kane.

He was huge, for one thing. He stood many

inches taller than her dad, and he was broad shouldered with it. He had really nice milk chocolate colored skin, and his hair was glossy black, streaked with some silver strands. The silver matched his eyes. He wore black clothes as well, and he looked to be Gardina's complete opposite. It was hard to believe that they were related at all.

His eyes fell on her face and warmed as he smiled. "Yours?" he asked Niall and Selene alike. His deep voice perfectly suited the rest of his appearance.

"Your cousin's," Niall retorted dryly.

Kane slowly lifted a brow. "This ought to be good." He stepped back. "Come in. And thank you for coming as quickly as you could."

"I needed your aid for Kae as well," Selene admitted. "The timing was perfect. There's a lot of trouble right now, Kane. Ghosty's manor has been burned to the ground."

He went very still. "What?" He visibly bit back a curse as he shut the door with his cane before limping slowly toward the family room. "Start at the top."

"Gardina found a Devoted. One of, hmm, compatible hormones." Selene was tactful only because of the tiny ears listening avidly. "His name is Matthias Logan. He was the Commander of the Armed Forces for Rikan. Kae was innocent blood spilled during the current war. Gardina urged him to bring Kae to her so she could protect them both." She sighed as she sat down on a couch. "And, of course, I came out to heal Kae."

Niall put Kae down on the couch so he could help Kane sit in a chair. His stomach was already churning at the idea of how much a mess Kane's leg might be if it was incapacitating him that much. "Suppose it coulda stayed that simple, but some Bleeder of a hunter came out looking for Logan, and Kae. Kept me and Selene from fightin' by bringing silver arrows. Torched the manor when Gardina would not reveal where she'd hid her charges."

"That doesn't make sense." Kane frowned. "People defect all the time. What would they care if this Commander Logan left for neutral territory in Coronia?"

"I have suspicions," Selene admitted. "I will speak of them soon enough. There are more pressing matters right now. While Gardina and Matthias are trying to seek sanctuary, we have been caring for Kae. She will be Matthias' daughter soon enough."

"I want Gardina for my mommy," Kae told Kane very seriously.

He hid a smile. "I don't blame you. She was much like a mother to me as well. She never seems to remember we're just cousins. Distant cousins, even."

Niall snorted. "Friend, when it comes to Ghosty, family is all that matters. Don't matter how much or little blood. She decided you're family, and that's that." He eyed Kane's leg and cane equally. "Got a bit too close?"

"Far too close," he confirmed. "I didn't see the trap until too late. Took my ankle and a chunk of my leg alike. No other doctor or healer has been able to do anything for me short of holding the pain at bay. I don't mind keeping a limp. I don't even mind phantom pains. I just want my mobility back. I'm too damned young to be put down this way."

At forty, he was only just entering the prime of his life. He was actually at the normal age when a Devoted would become an Etyrnal if that was their wish. Niall had been thirty-nine. Matthias was on the younger side at thirty-four, but extenuating circumstances could always exist. Kane seemed to have extenuating ones going the other way, and it deeply bothered Selene. If anyone deserved to be an Etyrnal, it was the man who had dedicated his life to protecting those who stayed on the side of good while removing those who went to the side of evil.

"I will aid you, if you can aid me," Selene said only. She gestured to Kae. "Let's get the formalities done. This is Kaeleigh Logan, or Kae for short. As we said, she is Matthias' adopted daughter. She is half-Fae."

"Well!" Kane's eyes brightened with amusement and warmth as he looked at Kae. "It's nice to meet you, Kae. I am Vladimir Kane. Just Kane will suffice. Only Gardina has ever gotten away with calling me by my first name."

"Nice to meet you," she countered politely. She quickly covered her mouth to hide a yawn. "I'm tired," she complained to Niall. She crawled into his arms and snuggled close. "Can I nap?"

"Yeah. Go to sleep, little mite." He studied her face for a moment after she had slipped asleep and then sighed. "I'd swear she was supposed to be my Devoted, but she was born the night of a Water Moon, not Millennium!"

"Kae is . . . complicated," Selene said at last. "I *think* she was supposed to be your Devoted, but she was born prematurely.

Almost two months early, and that shifted her from the Millennium Moon to the Water Moon. It's not unusual, in fact. I've known two other half-Fae in my life, and they were also early births. There is a great deal of destiny at play in this entire scenario."

"Who were her parents?" Kane murmured.

Selene smiled at him. "Ah, there's that quick wit again! Her father was Human and her mother was Fae. They lived in Desertia. When I asked Kae about her birth family, she said that her parents died a year ago. Her brother was actually her foster guardian." She looked at Kae's family mark. "That mark is not hers by birth. It was the mark of her foster family since they were going to adopt her. It already shows signs of changing again. It won't settle until Matthias and Gardina decide on their shared mark."

"And Logan? Is it connected to why he is being hunted?"

Selene hesitated. "His presence on the Rikan battlefield was no surprise to me. His role within it was. You see, because there is only one Ghost Etyrnal, there was only one child born that one night when the Ghost Moon was full by itself. The Ghost Moon negates the powers of Life and Death equally. Matthias Logan was that child. And yet . . . if you look at the records, there is no listing of Matthias Logan being born that night. Strangely enough, Matthias Logan was born the night *before* the full Ghost Moon. The child born the night of the full Ghost Moon was actually Tobias Sovereign."

"Son-of-a-bitch," Niall muttered. "That's why Feran and Richards were watchin' Matthias. They've known all along who he is."

"At the least, they knew it from the moment Gardina made contact with him. Only Tobias Sovereign could have been the Devoted of the Gray Etyrnal. They no doubt want him to find the Greater Sovereign Runic. Feran wants to be immortal." Selene made a helpless gesture. "There is nothing we can do to help with any of this until Gardina sends word to us. We might only make matters worse. Gardina does not know Matthias' true identity, and certainly he does not as well. I couldn't just tell them my suspicions. Ignorance might be safest for them."

"Yeah, but if this is all destiny," Niall retorted, "then ain't nothin' going to stop them from findin' out the truth. And fixin' whatever is wrong. Something has to be."

Kane's eyes lingered on Kae's sleeping figure. "Centuries of feuding, perhaps. Gardina nearly married a Sovereign prince, remember? Maybe the right one had not yet been born. Drop in a war with Desertia that the rightful prince can end by retaking his throne and offering an alliance, and the countries will all be united. Of course, it might all just be for Gardina's happy ending."

Selene's eyes closed as she understood what he was saying. "I had feared that."

Niall scowled. "Now what?"

"She can't transform Matthias. She is not a normal Etyrnal, my love." She smoothed a hand over his arm when horror filled his eyes. "But if Matthias is Tobias and he takes up the Sovereign Runic, then he will be a True Etyrnal as well. And by being a Devoted, he will make the transition seamlessly. Our mother goddess and father god love Ghosty more than any other Etyrnal. She will have happiness."

"In the meantime," Kane reached over and took Kae from Niall, "we might as well ensure her family is well-cared for. Someone recently noted that she puts family first. Children in particular. She's something of their personal guardian, I think. Niall, there are sleeping herbs in the kitchen. We want Kae down as much as she can be. She'll sleep off the surgery as well as recovery and wake intact."

Niall immediately fetched them and helped feed them to Kae. He then turned his back as he saw Kane drawing a dagger. "If it's all the same," he muttered, "I won't watch. I don't trust my bedside manner. I can't stand her in pain. Let's not see how I handle seein' her blood!"

Neither Selene nor Kane begrudged him that. Kae might not *actually* be Niall's Devoted, but she was close enough to it to make things tricky for the Dark Etyrnal. Selene removed Kae's loose tunic and even Kane grimaced when he saw the mess of Kae's back. "I'm glad you brought her here. This is bad. Niall, do *not* look."

"I need a drink," Niall muttered. He stalked into the kitchen. If there was anything he was glad he hadn't had to give up on his transformation, it was alcohol. Giving up the sun hadn't been a big deal. Booze was another story.

It did not take long for Kane to very gently split Kae's skin open so that Selene could coax her wings into unfurling. They opened enough to emerge from her back but remained in a curled position. That was not unusual. They would open entirely once she had fully recovered. A few days' rest would take care of that. Selene healed and sealed up the split skin and it soon looked as if the wings had always been there. A few lingering scars could be seen where the wings connected to the skin of her back, but that was, again, not unusual for half-Fae. It would have been worse without Kane.

"Niall?" Selene called. "Bring the alcohol for Kane and then take Kae upstairs and get her cleaned up. Nothing is bleeding now; it's just lingering stains."

Her husband walked into the room and still winced when he saw the mess. He handed the bottle to Kane and scooped up his little Fae. She didn't stir as he carried her out of the room, and he sighed as he saw Snacks pacing. "Alright, feline. Y'can come along. Don't you be hoggin' her bed again."

Kane looked at Selene and said solemnly, "He's adorable."

She bit her lip to hide a smile. "Shh! You know Etyrnals have good hearing. Now let's see your leg." She helped him shift position until his leg was braced on the low table and rolled up his pant leg to reveal the injury. Even after a thousand years of being a healer, some things could still horrify her. She turned her head away briefly. "By the gods, Kane." She braced her shoulders and turned back.

Entire chunks of flesh had been torn away from his ankle and leg alike, and only a magical seal prevented it from continuing to spill blood. There was no scabbing over this wound. Selene's best hope was to rebuild as much tissue as she could and let the rest become scarring. He would assuredly limp, but she could at least make sure he got rid of the cane. Knowing him, he would even find a way to hide the limp.

She briefly fetched hot water and new bandages. She then got to work gingerly removing the seal. "I recommend drinking that alcohol now and perhaps indulging enough to get a bit drunk. Also, cussing might be helpful. This will *not* be pleasant. I need you conscious for this else I'd just knock you out like we did to Kae."

"I can handle things." The first lick of pain from the hot water made his breath promptly hiss out on a string of curses that would impress even Niall. "Never mind." He took a healthy drink from the bottle. "I think I'll get drunk."

Chapter Fourteen

Matthias woke slowly and a bit painfully. His lungs felt slightly scratchy, and for the life of him he could not figure out why. Memory returned in a rush and he sat upright on a jerk. It was pitch dark wherever he was and he could not see anything. He patted at his hip and found his gun was gone; Niall would kill him. He got to his feet and carefully edged forward. His hands encountered bars and he knew it was a dungeon cell. He felt along the cage door until he found the wall and a torch with flint dangling from it. Two strikes lit the torch and filled the area with dim light.

The first thing he saw was Gardina curled up on the other cot. His shoulders relaxed slightly. He vaguely remembered her slipping in and out of his mind over the last day, trying to coax him awake, but he just hadn't been able to respond. His last coherent memory was an odd red glow as he had been on the cusp of drowning.

He walked over to Gardina and leaned over to wake her, and he froze as he saw bandages over her bare shoulder. He roughly jerked the blanket back and a pained sound tangled in his chest at the sight of the bloodstained bandages covering her delicate body. "Ghosty," he managed to say hoarsely.

"Matt?" She tried to turn over and winced hard as her body protested the movement. "I can't move."

Fingers trembling, he gingerly reached out and helped her move into a sitting position. She was much paler than usual, and misery lined her darkened eyes. His gaze lowered to the choker around her neck, and fury stirred. "What is that thing?"

"Fae artifact. Long story short, it blocks Etyrnal power. It almost killed me."

"It looks like someone else tried that!"

"It was both. The choker nearly shattered my Runic, and then Feran tried to beat me senseless. Remember the 'cause you a trauma to make you remember your childhood' thing? They thought perhaps this would traumatize you enough for that." She searched his eyes and managed a smile. "You look more pissed off than traumatized. If you were a healer instead of a warrior, it might be different. They don't know you very well, I guess."

He eased onto the cot beside her and framed her face with a shaking hand. "I'm still slightly traumatized. Damn it, Gardina! You shouldn't have even gone near them! You could have stayed here where it was safe!"

She cupped his cheek. "They threatened you. And I knew I could not die. I admit, I got closer than I expected, but I came out. General Richards stopped the abuse and even tended to my wounds. He is . . ." she sought the word, "conflicted. He is not a threat. And perhaps we need only to wait out Feran. He has only two weeks left."

Something ancient and powerful filled his eyes. The red in the pupil was more potent than ever. "He will die by my hand."

"Then we need to get out of here. Can you get this thing off me? Once I go into specter form, I can start healing. I'll be able to abandon most of the physical pain. The only physical sensations I've ever found that follow me into specter form is my desire for you."

He studied the choker for a clasp but found none. On a burst of furious strength, he merely ripped it apart. As soon as she was free of it, she went translucent. The bandages did not go with her, and they dropped free around her body. Another rumble that was a stifled roar of rage echoed from Matthias' chest as he saw in horrific detail just how badly she had been hurt.

Blessedly, he could see some of the smaller wounds already beginning to seal and disappear. It also dawned on him that she was very naked, and he scowled. He spotted the clothes on the end of the bed and pointedly held them out. If she couldn't feel pain, then there was nothing stopping her from covering up. "I have a feeling that naked ghosts would scare people more."

"And you're a jealous man." She didn't argue, though. She went physical to grab the clothes and they turned translucent with her. Seeing the question, she explained, "Certain cloth types can't shift with me. They need to be really light in order to shift. Bandages are thick stuff." Once dressed, she drifted easily through the bars. "I'll get the keys."

He waited patiently for her to return, and once he was freed, he grabbed the torch. "We need to get out of here, as you said. We need a strategy if I'm to kill Feran." He studied his lover's face. "And I suspect you may know more than you've thus far told me."

"I only just figured out what is really going on," she admitted softly. "But this is not the time or place, and I'm in no condition to hold you together. It's going to devastate you."

He blew out a hard breath. "That bad?"

"Worse, probably. Let's find an escape route."

Something flickered through his mind and he frowned. "There's a secret escape down here. I just thought of it. Weird. I've never been down here." He stopped breathing for a moment. "Or have I? Shit. Maybe I was traumatized by you after all."

"Then we *really* need to get out. I'll find the secret escape." She began drifting in and out of the walls until she found one that led not to another room but to a long tunnel. She moved down it enough to be sure it led out and then went back for her Devoted. She pointed at the wall. "That one."

He began to examine the bricks for a sign of something unusual. There had to be something. He found it in an odd piece of mortar. When he pulled on it, he dislodged a brick. Removal of the brick revealed a hidden switch. That switch opened the wall enough to allow him to pass through. He put the brick back and ducked inside the tunnel, and it closed behind him a moment later.

The torch provided enough light to see as they made their way quickly down the tunnel. It was cold, damp, and eerie. He could nearly hear the screams buried in the walls, and more flickers of memory moved across his mind's eye. For a moment, he thought he heard someone calling his name but it wasn't his name. He just knew they were calling him. His heart began to beat dully in his chest.

His unease was not aided by the fact that he just seemed to know which routes through the catacombs to take. Gardina looked at his face and cursed her inability to hold him. Trying to do so would only upset him more because it would cause her pain.

They eventually reached a dead end and a ladder, and she went up first. She returned to give him the go-ahead, and he climbed up to the hatch. He found himself at the bottom of an old well, and there was another ladder to climb out. The well exited into the Deserted Woods around the castle, and the woods stretched for miles in many directions.

Abandoned woodsmen's cottages were scattered across the Woods. They passed up several in their efforts to put more distance between them and the castle. They finally located one that would be easy to disguise, and Gardina used her Runic to surround it with thick fog. The fog shone eerily red in the light of the full Sovereign Moon overhead. The Ghost and Water Moons had been replaced by others, and the

Sovereign would leave within two weeks. The symbolism was not lost on Gardina.

There was nothing inside the cottage except an old bed, a stove, and a broken window. It was surprisingly clean overall, though, and little dust clung to the corners. Someone had used it recently. Matthias lit the stove for warmth and light though he did fasten the curtains into place to keep out the moonlight.

Gardina perched on the side of the bed without actually touching it, and he looked her over critically. The wounds were indeed disappearing quickly. By morning, they might be gone entirely. "Do you want to talk now?" he asked her quietly as he sat beside her.

She shook her head. "Tomorrow morning. I'm not up to it right now. You're going to need me, Matt."

"I've always needed you." He lifted a hand, then dropped it. He wanted to touch her more than anything. Wanted to hold her. She had gone too close, been reminded too sharply, about her half-dead side. She needed the life he could bring her. "How much do you hurt?"

"Let's see." She solidified and let out a breath. "Actually, it's not as bad as it was. My ribs hurt the most, but I think they were cracked. It's more an ache now than a pain. I've always been a fast healer, even without my specter form." Her lips trembled as he pulled her onto his lap and tenderly enfolded her in his arms. "I needed that."

"So did I." He buried his face in her hair. "How did this happen, Gardina? In such a short time, you've become one of the most important things in my life. It can't be just because I am your Devoted. This is far more than just compatible hormones. More than love."

"Eternity." She smoothed her fingers over his face. "It's there between us. Even though you don't have it, it's there. Love that can last forever. The sweetest part of being an Etyrnal." Very softly, she added, "The gift from the gods."

"Oh ho, someone sounds like a believer."

"Maybe a little. I want proof though."

"The eternal optimist wants proof."

"Optimism doesn't mean I'm stupid."

"Fair enough." He tilted her chin up and kissed her warmly until she sighed and melted against him. "Proof enough?" he asked huskily.

"I forgot the question. Try again." She was smiling when he kissed her again. While she very much looked forward to giving him his Runic and making him an Etyrnal, she still dreaded what it may do to him emotionally. "I need more rest, Matt."

"I know." He turned and gently put her down. She turned translucent again and he went to muffle the light of the stove. He made his way back to her side in the darkness and laid down beside her. "I want to hold you."

"You can."

"Not without hurting you."

"No, you can." Even the dark, her smile was visible. "I can possess you again. Actually, that might even help me heal faster. I wouldn't have to expend any energy at all. It'll also make us both feel as if we're holding each other." Softer, she added, "I've possessed people before, but it never felt as . . . intimate as it did with you. I think our souls are actually touching."

"It feels the same as when we make love. I noticed that later." He trailed a finger down her face though neither felt it. "Go ahead. I like holding you however I can."

She lightly brushed her lips against his before disappearing into his body. That warm intimacy filled him and he closed his eyes on a sigh. He had slept for a long time and yet he was still a bit tired. Apparently, near drowning could be hell on the body.

He woke a bit abruptly the next morning as light slipped around the blinds and fell on his face. He knew even before he opened his eyes that Gardina had stopped possessing him. He looked around the room and found her standing near the window. She was opening the blinds and the morning sun illuminated the fact that she looked perfectly healthy again. There was no evidence of the torture she had endured.

He got to his feet and walked over to tug her into his arms for a hungry kiss. Her skin warmed under his touch and she floated up to wrap her arms around his neck. Feeling her soft and alive made the lingering icy fear let him go at last. "Holding you isn't quite the same as *holding* you," he murmured thickly against her lips. "And if we weren't on a deadline, I would be suggesting we see how durable that bed really is."

She trailed her fingers over his lips. "I think someone has come to enjoy many things he missed out on by being at war."

"I blame you." He stole another kiss. "You make everything better just by being there." He slowly and reluctantly released her. "And since we're both hale and hearty, I think we had better have our discussion about what has been really going on."

She drew him over to the bed and urged him to sit down. She knelt in front of him and took his hands with hers. She brought them to her lips for a moment and then let out a long breath. "You are not Matthias Logan."

Some of the color began to leave his face. He was not stupid. "Then who am I?" he asked softly.

"Your birth name is Tobias Sovereign." She held tighter to his hands when they began to shake. "You are the rightful heir to the throne of Rikan. You had an older sister who should have been queen, but you are the only surviving heir. I've looked to be sure. I should have made the connection sooner, to be honest. When I found you, I just never questioned the circumstances."

It dawned. "I was the only child born that night," he said softly. "And if you look at the records of births the night of the full Ghost Moon, it would say the name of the child born."

"The real Matthias was born the night *before* the moon. Only Tobias was born the night of the full moon." Her gaze lowered. "I am sorry. It must have been me finding you that put you onto Feran's radar.

Only Tobias Sovereign could have been the Devoted of the Gray Etyrnal, and if *you* are my Devoted, then you must be Tobias."

"Then how did I become Matthias?" he asked quietly. "I thought they found the bodies of the prince and princess."

"This is speculation, but I suspect that the real Matthias was used as a decoy. You were of the same age, and it would not be difficult to make him look like the prince. They would have just needed to change his family mark, and if he was made a member of the family, that would have done it." She smoothed her hand over the traces effects on his lower arm. "As soon as he was dead and therefore your family was dead, your mark disappeared. There would be nothing to say you weren't Matthias. You certainly couldn't say otherwise."

He drew a ragged breath. "How did you figure this out?"

"It was a few things. Something about you had always felt strangely familiar to me. I chalked it up to the Ghost Moon. But that time when I was telling you about how the Sovereign could only by used by the royal bloodline . . . you made a quip about what Leo had said. It was *verbatim* what Alexander had said. It made me look again." She reached up and skimmed her fingers over the corner of his eyes. "Your pupils have a red hue. Only exposure to a Greater Runic would do that. Your green eyes are a match for the royal bloodline."

"What made you *sure*?"

She covered the mark on her chest and reached inside. She drew out the Sovereign Runic and held it out on her palm. It began to glow softly red the moment it was near Matthias. "I found this imbedded in your family mark when I pulled you out of the ocean. It had been hidden inside you, and it came out when you fought to live. Someone hid it inside you for safety. It was right there under everyone's noses all this time."

He slowly reached out and took the Runic from her. It felt familiar in his hand. There were still questions to be answered, but the biggest ones had finally come clear. "Maybe that's why you liked Alexander," he murmured. "A prelude to us."

"Royal blood does breed strong."

He took a long breath. "You know what my biggest feeling is in all this?" She shook her head and he cupped her cheek with his free hand. "Relief. If I fuse this Runic, I will be a Dark Etyrnal. I will have eternity to share with you. That's the only thing that really matters to me. Maybe this is the way it was always meant to fall. You can't transform me, but it doesn't matter now." He let out the breath he had taken. "Anything I need to know before I fuse this?"

"Don't tense up and fight. Let it take you as it will, and if you need to sleep, do it." She went and closed the blinds again. "You won't be able to test your power until nightfall, and therefore this is the best time to do the transformation anyway. You will have time to recover. I don't expect it to take long, though. You have been preparing for this all along by being my Devoted."

"Is that all?" He combed his fingers through her hair when she sat beside him.

"Well, you're in for some changes on waking, that's for sure. Again, you've been prepping for this all along, and quickly. I will hunt while you are resting, and I'll be able to feed you when you wake. You'll need fresh blood as well for the first day or two, and it really wouldn't be safe to hit the hospital while you're an outlaw anyway." She admitted softly, "It is possible that *this* will be what jogs out your memories."

"I have you to hold me together. And having

eternity makes it worthwhile." He took a breath to brace himself and then closed his hand hard around the Runic. The small globe knew that for the signal it was and began to glow brightly. He slowly opened his hand and watched as the globe pushed its way deeper into his palm. It didn't hurt as much as he might have expected.

The back of his hand began to burn with just enough force to sting and he turned his hand over to see the mark of Sovereign appearing. It glowed dark red against his tanned skin. He could feel a sort of odd sensation in his internal organs, but nothing unpleasant. At most, he had a strange feeling he might get the hiccups. What really clued him in that he was changing was that he winced hard when a bit of light snuck in around the blinds.

"Oops!" Gardina hastily refastened the blinds and added more fog around the cottage to help. "Yeah, that's going to stick for a while," she warned as she returned to his side. "You'll need to rebuild your endurance. You won't burst into flames or any such silly thing, but your eyes will be happy to remind you that the sun is no longer your friend. It would probably be best if we shift to a nocturnal schedule so you can actually enjoy your power."

The world never truly slept. Humans were a relatively fifty-fifty split as to whether they lived nocturnally or diurnally. Etyrnals were somewhat secretive and kept to themselves—kept them from risking attachments to things and people they might lose—but they were always able to join any part of the society they wished. He focused his suddenly tired eyes on Gardina and asked, "How many Etyrnals are there?"

She began to gently help him lie down. "A few thousand. Now it's a few thousand and one." She feathered a kiss over his forehead. "Sleep, my love. Let your body process. It's been run ragged recently." She drew the blanket over him and let out a relieved breath when he fell asleep. He had definitely taken the transformation well. She had seen some Devoted all but fall over unconscious as their body demanded recovery time. It was tiring to change species.

He stayed peacefully asleep while she left briefly to hunt. She took care to feed a bit more than usual because she needed to care for her Devoted as well, but there were several magically potent people in the closest city. They would never even notice the difference.

She monitored Matthias the entire day. She supposed she ought to start calling him by his birth name, but it just wasn't his name anymore. It would be silly to expect him to start using a name that he had only used for the first three years of his life. Besides. She rather liked the sound of 'Gardina Logan' more than 'Gardina Sovereign.' It was too much a mouthful. Arguably, they could both take a new last name, but she liked the idea of honoring the boy who had sacrificed himself for his prince. Matthias would too.

Curiosity had her grabbing the broken mirror off the wall and taking out outside where she could see clearer. She propped it against the wall and tugged down her tunic to see the family mark on her back shoulder. It still showed as the royal crest of the Campbell royal family, but she could see where parts of it were fading. She and Matthias would need to decide on a symbol for their new family so that Kae could share it as well. She had an idea already, in fact. It would be symbolic.

The sun was beginning to set when Matthias started to stir at last. She lit the lamp with one of her matches and left it low. The new light was enough to wake him wholly, and he blinked rapidly after opening his eyes. "Okay, that's different." He jolted at the sound of his voice. "And that! Am I shouting?"

She bit her lip but a giggle emerged anyway. "It's night now. Your powers have settled and are stirring. Part of those powers are heightened senses. Come the dawn, you'll go to normal range again, but it will feel more like you've been stifled now that you've been enhanced." She leaned over him. "Welcome to eternity," she offered softly.

Wonder filled his face as he slowly reached up to touch her face. She just somehow seemed more beautiful to his sharpened eyes. He had never noticed before, but she had very faint freckles over her nose that enchanted him. His gaze dropped and he spotted the pulse beating in her neck. Hunger awoke violently and he felt his incisors lengthen. He gingerly touched them but it felt strangely comfortable.

"Are we hungry?" she teased. Her breath came out on a slightly breathless giggle as he sat up with his newly enhanced speed and yanked her onto his lap. His mouth closed hotly over her neck and she shivered in delight. "I overfed," she said huskily. "That can be pretty dangerous. Risks driving an Etyrnal mad with bloodlust. Better help me come back to a safer level."

"How deep do I bite?"

"You'll see. Instinct takes over." She urged his head closer. "You'll also be able to taste how much you're taking. When you taste an odd sweetness, you'll know you've taken enough for yourself. If it turns sour, you'll know you've taken too much from me. Everyone is a little different. That's why we can taste the limits."

It felt only the littlest bit odd to him. He truly had been preparing for his transformation all along. He nipped just hard enough to break skin and the first taste of her blood was startlingly tasty. He lifted his head quickly and saw the little drop of gray running down her skin. He lightly touched it and then brought his finger to his lips. "Gray?" he asked huskily.

"Yours is black now. A Light Etyrnal is white." The little ache in her neck matched the ache growing low in her body. She *needed* to feel him sinking his teeth into her skin. "Matt." The ache was in her voice.

He couldn't resist. He bent his head again and hesitated for only a moment before sinking in his teeth. That familiar firestorm of erotic lust and hunger surged through his body. The little moan she made did nothing to help his control. She tasted *incredible*. He would probably like most bloods (he had never been a picky eater), but hers was cake among bread. A sudden hint of a different sweetness touched his tongue and he slowly lifted his head. Desire made them both tremble hard.

Dazed, wickedly aroused, she stared at him. "Wow," she breathed thickly. "That's as good as doing the biting. We're going to have *fun* in our eternity." She shivered as he delicately licked the bite mark to close it. "Ooh. Quick learner."

"You know me. I'm happy to learn anything you want to teach. Think this bed will hold up to some bouncing?"

"Depends on who's on top."

The bed proved relatively sturdy, thankfully. The floor would have been too cold (and dirty), and waiting wasn't an option. There had been too many brushes with death, too many scares, to resist embracing life. That alone would have had them all over each other without throwing in newly made eternity and compatible hormones between Etyrnals. Matthias tucked his hands under his head and noted ruefully, "We may need to plan out eating in private if that's going to keep happening."

"You'll learn to control it more as you age, just like any other desire." She snuggled closer against his side. "Definitely still best to plan on alone time, what with us raising a daughter in the house, but if it isn't feasible, then we'll be fine. Besides, it's just us. You bite anyone else and you won't notice much of anything. In fact, you'll discover the idea of going for anyone else's neck will actually be kind of repugnant."

He thought about it and found she was right. He loathed the idea of getting anywhere near anyone's neck but hers. "Hence why you mentioned the wrist."

"We save the neck for lovers. It's too personal otherwise." She gently smoothed her hand across his chest and down to rest over the scar on his ribs.

He released a ragged breath. "I had been having nightmares. I was sleeping in my parents' room. Suddenly there were screams and fires. Soldiers burst in and just . . ." He shuddered. "I'm not sure I wholly comprehended what had happened. They didn't see me in there. I ran out and went to my room to hide. My nanny found me. One of the soldiers came in after her. The sword went through her body and across mine. Another servant—his name was William—knocked the soldier out and grabbed me. He rushed me to another room. We only had minutes. Matthias was there. We looked alike, actually."

She held him tighter. "They told you to accept him as your brother."

"He was my best friend." His eyes closed. "He almost was my brother. I still didn't even understand what was happening. I was happy when I saw he had my family mark. They separated us and said we were escaping. We went out through the dungeon." The red in his pupils flickered. "We were followed. Only a few of us made it out and into the city. My last memory is of tripping and falling flat on the stone sidewalk. I woke up to amnesia. I was told I was Matthias Logan, the son of a servant, and one of five survivors."

"And since your mark had been erased, there was no one to say otherwise. William must have grabbed the Runic and passed it to you for safety while you were out. You wouldn't know you had it even if you woke with memories. Your amnesia must have seemed a blessing to the other survivors. Are any of them still around?"

"The boy who went into the orphanage with me, but I don't think he knew what had happened to me. He was with another servant escaping another route. It was William, myself, and another together. The other person was a chef. I don't know what happened to him or William. For all I know, only

William realized that 'Matthias' was actually 'Tobias'."

She was inclined to agree. The fewer people who knew the truth, the safer he would be. She very much hoped William was still alive. She wanted to thank him for his bravery and loyalty, and for helping ensure her Devoted lived. "Well, what next? You wanted to kill Feran for what he had done recently, but I think we both know that's also an echo of what he had done already. You are the last member of the Sovereign royal family. You have earned blood right."

"What are our options?"

"Hmm." She sat up beside him. "Charging the palace and making a big ruckus. Going to the frontlines and having you announce your birthright and stop the war in a single swoop. Unlocking the full potential of Sovereign Runic and *then* going to said frontlines or charging the door."

"What's the most likely to work?"

"Well, unlocking the full potential would need to be done sooner or later and it would give access to all of the Runic's abilities now. Full potential of a Runic can only be done by taking it to the place where it fell to the land from the moon." She tapped a finger against her lips. "Arguably, we could safely charge the palace, though the frontlines might be easier. When I went hunting, I got a feel for things. Seems that you're almost in charge of the country without anyone knowing who you are."

He stared at her. "What?"

"The 'war' is kind of paused right now. The soldiers refuse to take orders from anyone but their commander, and the other side is content to let it stand. The people are threatening mutiny against Feran unless the war ends. They believe in their Commander Logan; if he left, there must be a reason. No one in Rikan wants to take up the bounty on you." She smiled. "I suppose that is the other sign that you are of royal blood. Even if you weren't, if you stormed the castle and removed Feran, you'd be happily crowned king before the day was done."

It was humbling and daunting alike. "Like your people and you," he murmured.

"And Desertia and the Vargas bloodline. Maybe whatever draws Greater Runics to us is the thing that makes us natural leaders." Thinking about that made her add, "There *is* one other link in this chain that I'm only suspicious of and don't yet have proof for, but is probably true with how everything else has fallen. I'm beginning to see what the outcome of all of this will be."

"And that is?"

"Peace on our landmass." She huffed out a breath. "Let's get going to the Crypt of Kings where the Sovereign fell to the land, and I'll tell you along the way. It'll make as much sense to you as it does to me. It kinda ties up everything neatly." She winced. "And if I'm right, I'll finally give in and concede that, yeah, there are gods. It will be proof enough that there has to be some sort of higher power at work."

He hid a smile. "Are we at the point of being too complicated for coincidence?"

"That's one way of putting it," she groused.

Chapter Fifteen

The Crypt of Kings was located two miles west of the cabin and tucked into a thickly lined area of woods. As the name implied, it was the final resting place of the Sovereign royal family. Arguably, it could be called the Crypt of Kings and Queens since Rikan had been ruled equally by both, but it was a much bigger mouthful.

The closer to the Crypt that Matthias and Gardina drew, the thicker the presence of the undead felt. Spirits and specters lingered just out of range but could still be sensed. Even Matthias could see them clearly, since he still maintained his sensitivity to Gray power thanks to his birth under the Ghost Moon.

Thinking it, he murmured, "Maybe that was another reason. To allow me to see you. If I had no innocence, then I shouldn't see you. Yet I do."

She was drifting along at his side, and at that she slipped her hand into his. "I am *your* innocence. You would have seen me anyway." She gestured to the woods as a whole. "These are echoes. They are not truly ghosts. They cannot possess anyone. They merely guard the Crypt out of respect for the dead within. I've been here once or twice over the centuries."

"That's how you knew it was where the Sovereign had landed." He studied her curiously. "Did you unlock your Runic?"

"I did. About, hmm, five years after I gained it."

"Where was it located?"

She smiled up at him. "Almost right where my ancestor built the castle. I had to go down under the catacombs." She winced wryly. "Forcefully turned me into my specter form for the first time. I scared myself as badly as I scared my sister who had gone with me. Sadly, I don't know where any of the others landed. Odds are, they would be easy to find if we had to try. They tend to correlate to the power of the Runic."

"Good to know." He looked around the woods and found himself fascinated anew at how clearly he could see. He just *felt* stronger, too. His lungs and heart seemed incapable of speeding up and making him breathless. Well, unless he happened to be admiring his lover, but even Etyrnals couldn't resist nature.

She grinned impishly. "If anything, Etyrnals get to enjoy nature *more*." She sighed gustily. "It has been far too quiet. By now, they have to know we're gone. They would have to assume you were traumatized by the sight of me and therefore got your memories back and therefore knew where the Runic was and therefore would need to empower it, so right about now, I'm expecting criminals promised immunity for handing you over to burst out of the trees and demand you surrender and me to not make any funny moves."

They both stopped walking as they felt a familiar chill that meant danger crept close. It was sharper than ever inside Matthias, and he realized with some surprise that *all* of his senses had been enhanced. A soft rustling through bushes started at only an Etyrnal level of sound and then grew louder until several ragged figures burst out to surround the two Etyrnals. They wore the familiar uniforms that marked them as criminals.

The one in the front barked, "Surrender, Logan! Our immunity rides on bringing you back alive." He aimed a gun at Gardina. "Don't make any funny moves."

"I wanted you to be wrong," Matthias groused at Gardina.

She grinned. "Niall says that a lot too." A quick perusal of the enemy told her that no one carried silver weapons of any sort. She was bit disappointed, actually, that Feran was stupid enough to think Matthias would have the Runic and not fuse it. He apparently knew nothing about Runics, Etyrnals, or even love itself. She actually began to pity him more than she disliked him.

She could have very easily taken care of the problem herself with any number of creative things. Instead, she held up her hands and took a step back. "Sure thing. I don't feel like doing anything strenuous anyway. I've only just gotten over my second brush with death. You don't need to worry about me at all."

The criminals were at least smart enough to sense something off. It only dawned on them why she was so meekly giving in when they spotted a dark glow sweeping up around Matthias' body. They turned sharply as one and found him watching them with a sardonic brow lifted. He was holding his right hand up, and the mark of Sovereign was obvious. "He's a True Etyrnal!" one of the criminals croaked out. "Shit! We don't have silver weapons! Get out of here!"

They collectively scrambled to run. Without guilt, Matthias calmly fired bolts of Dark power after them. Each blast was precisely aimed and strong enough to kill. While the Sovereign's true power lay in its ability to influence and manipulate others, it could still be a weapon. All Light Runics could use raw Light power just as all Dark Runics could use raw Dark power. In that manner, all Runics could be weapons.

As the bodies settled, he dusted off his hands and turned to Gardina. "That was strangely satisfying. It's about time that I could protect you the way you've protected me." He cocked his head curiously. "Does an Etyrnal stop feeling compelled to protect and shelter their Devoted after the Devoted becomes an Etyrnal?"

"Hmm, yes and no. It diminishes under normal circumstances but never goes away. I would always fuss over you even if we weren't lovers. I would continue to fuss over you until I had another Devoted to focus on. You would then always be dear to me, but I would know you no longer needed me and I no longer needed you." She smiled. "I will never have another Devoted, so you're stuck with me fussing for a long time. You, on the other hand, might get a dose of your own medicine eventually and have one of your own. Imagine how it felt to get Kae and multiply it by ten."

He winced. "Guess it would serve me right, as it has served many Etyrnals in the past. What about

Niall? When's he going to get his?"

She grinned. "I suspect he already is. I think Kae might be his Devoted."

He started laughing. "Couldn't happen to a nicer guy!" He tucked her under his arm again as they started deeper into the woods. They were not far from the Crypt.

Having never been to a crypt of any sort, he really hadn't known what to expect. Even if he had tried, he would have fallen short of the mark. The crypt entry was a small marble and brick building aboveground that had a staircase leading down into the crypt itself. It was warm and welcoming amid the spooky woods, and torches made of Light Runics burned eternally on the walls outside. The inside was a different story, and it dropped into immediate darkness.

As Gardina picked up an empty torch from the wall, she offered, "The darkness allows for the dead to rest peacefully. Remember when I mentioned spirits that linger after death because of the violent transition? Some do it even when the death is peaceful. They linger close to their bodies because it's familiar. To ensure they are at least able to rest, crypts and other burial grounds are kept in darkness."

He watched her draw out matches to light the torch, and something belatedly occurred to him. "Ghosty." He caught her shoulders and forced her to look at him. "You said you could carry only three things comfortably in your Runic. You had the Sovereign. You have your matches. Which did you sacrifice? Your log or your flute?"

"My flute," she admitted. She shook her head when he cursed. "It was just an instrument, Matt. I can get another one."

"I will buy it for you."

She had no desire to argue with him when he got that particular tone in his voice. "Alright. Besides, I'm okay. It was how I handled my loneliness." She smiled. "I have you now." She rose up to lightly kiss him and then offered the torch. "Kings first."

"Hey, I haven't been crowned. I'm still a prince. And I wasn't even supposed to be the heir, so you outrank me and should go first."

She snorted at that but obligingly went down the steps first. There was one bend to take them back under the entrance, ensuring the light from outside would stay there, and then the crypt opened up in all of its sprawling glory. Troughs of oil ran around the room, and he lit the end of one. A stream of fire swept around the edges and illuminated what lay within.

The crypt was made of the same marble and brick, and it seemed strangely immaculate and clean. Caskets and coffins made of stone were neatly lined along the walls and created aisles. Other rooms branched off where non-ruling members of the family were buried. Matthias walked slowly through the middle of the crypt and his boots were silent on the marble floor. He didn't feel unnerved to be there. He felt strangely peaceful. Death was never an end. The proof of it drifted along at his side.

They made their way through the coffins, and they skimmed over the names. One jumped out and Gardina stopped to lightly trace the letters. "Alexander Sovereign," she murmured. "When he was old, he called me to his side. He looked at me very seriously and said, 'Gardina, I'm sorry I could not love you the way you wanted. I hope someday there is someone who can.' He was a good man, a wonderful king, and an incredible warrior." She looked up at her lover. "You are so much like him, Matt."

He tugged her close for a moment before they continued through the chamber. Something about the place nagged at them both, but it wasn't until they reached the end and found the casket holding his father that he realized what was wrong. "There's no more room." He slowly looked around the crypt. "There's no more room. They would have to expand if there were more kings or queens to be buried here."

The moment he had taken his Runic, the Sovereign bloodline had effectively ended. It was another eerie reminder that perhaps there was more than a little destiny at play. Whether he ruled or not, the bloodline had ended. Either he would rule until the end of eternity, or another bloodline would take over. Gardina genuinely did not know what decision he had made. She would support him either way.

She spotted a tiny room off to the side, and a strange darkness lingered within. "There." She pointed. "I can see a red hue. That must be where you need to go." She shook her head with a smile when he looked at her. "This is for you to do. I will wait here."

He brushed his lips over hers before walking into the small room. It truly was small, and it held only a single casket. In a way, he was not at all surprised to walk closer and see his birth name engraved on it. Yet the one who slept within was not Tobias Sovereign. He gently rested a hand on the lid. "I literally owe you my life," he murmured. "You were my brother. You deserve to rest here."

The light around him suddenly turned gold in color, and he looked up sharply. Darkness flowed and gathered at the opposite wall and then parted to let a man walk forward. He was perhaps a bit shorter than Matthias, and he was strikingly gorgeous in appearance. He had thick coffee brown hair matched with verdant green eyes that rivaled the land for beauty. He smiled when he saw Matthias and said, "It's nice to see you when you are not almost dying." His voice suited the rest of him and sounded as velvety as darkness itself.

It took Matthias only a few moments to realize who he surely had to be looking upon. He stopped breathing. "You're . . . are you . . . Dark? The God of Darkness?"

Dark inclined his head. "Some call me Sun as well, but you are correct."

"I never understood that," he admitted. "You are the patron of Dark Etyrnals, but the sun is our enemy."

"Back in the beginning of it all, my beautiful Light was alone on this world. There were no shadows. Nothing to define the life she had brought forth. When I revealed myself to her, I created the sun to help control her light and bring forth darkness. In return, when I brought the night, she created the moons to control my darkness and bring forth light. That is why Etyrnals may be powerless when out of their domain but are not truly endangered. There is light in dark and dark in light." Softer, he added, "The sun is not an enemy of Dark Etyrnals. It is your protector. It gives you the weakness you need in order to rest. The moons are the same for Light Etyrnals. If you were constantly powerful, you would never rest peacefully."

It dawned. "Like Gardina. She doesn't dream."

"She cannot. She is Light and Dark both. She is Gray. By never being weakened, she can never truly rest. You had to be her Devoted in order to find her and to have the events happen as they have, but you could not be Gray. It is your darkness that shelters her, just as it will be Kae's light that illuminates her. Once the three of you are truly a family, Gardina will balance and she will rest. She will dream."

Matthias thought about everything and then asked softly, "Gardina is . . . is she your daughter?"

"Not *literally*, no, but it took me and Light working together to ensure she was born. Her lifeforce had such power! And the Ghost Moon negates Life and Death alike. When she was born, and we saw the beautiful shadowy, gray power inside her . . . we knew we would love her the most." He smiled. "Did you know that Gray power is not merely that of Ghost power? It is also the power of love. It is where light and dark come together."

"I believe it." Matthias let out a little breath. "And thank you. For explaining. You think you could hop out there and make my lover a believer again?"

Dark laughed. "Light has been gently pushing her forward all along, and you shook her recently when you accurately pointed out that she might not have actually gone far enough to reach Evermore. Light is with her now." He held out a hand. "Give me your Runic hand and I will unlock its potential for you."

Matthias obligingly took his hand. "Are there any other True Etyrnals out there?"

"Not yet."

Sensing it was another time where he shouldn't ask questions he didn't want the answer to, he said nothing more. He was still reeling a bit from what Gardina had explained about Kae. He should have known all along what was going on.

Out in the main crypt, Gardina contentedly

drifted between the caskets and coffins while she waited. It had taken hours of meditation for her to unlock her Runic. She had no idea how long it would take Matthias. She was fine with waiting. She was actually quite patient. Most Etyrnals either started that way or eventually evolved into it. It was hard to be impatient when you literally had forever to wait for things.

She was studying a casket for a queen from before even her time when everything went silvery around her. She froze, then slowly turned around. Her familiar ethereal companion stood just behind her. A little smile tugged at the other woman's lips. For the first time, Gardina actually noticed that the shadowy darkness around them did not obscure her companion. It caressed her legs while light effused her body. She could not be the spirit of the Ghost Runic. She was not Gray; she was wholly of the Light.

Gardina took a long breath. "Why?" It was all she asked.

"We love you." It was said just as simply.

Her hands curled into fists. "Then why did you let me continue to not believe? It hurt to stop believing. It hurts more to believe again."

"Pain makes you appreciate joy. We would not

be alive without it." She tenderly cupped Gardina's cheek. "In my eyes, you are my child. In Dark's eyes, you are his. We would not have wished any pain upon you, but it had to happen for you to truly be happy. You are our will on the land, little ghost. You help us maintain balance. Why do you think your logbook updates as it does?"

She scowled. "Darn it, I hate when Niall is right!" She raked a hand through her tangled white hair only to slowly stare at a lock. Her hair had always held a silvery tint in the light. Her eyes were gold in color. Even from her birth, she had been marked as blessed by the gods. Marked to be the Gray Etyrnal. She slowly looked at Light. "Is there really such a thing as destiny?"

"I prefer to think of it as ensuring the happiness of those I care for." She held out a hand. "Come with me. There is something you need to see."

After only a brief hesitation, Gardina took her hand. Light and dark equally blinded her for a brief moment. When her sight finally cleared, that familiar feeling of homecoming was stronger than ever. She blinked once, then twice, then slowly looked around with growing awe. She knew where she was. It looked exactly as she had once imagined it might. Evermore. It existed.

Fields upon fields upon *fields* of lush grass and colorful flowers stretched for ages around her. An immaculate blue sky was overlaid with shimmering silver clouds that allowed the blue to peek through. Ghostly spirits floated contentedly through the air. It was too beautiful, too peaceful, too *perfect* to belong to the realm of the living. It had to be the realm of the dead. The realm of Light and Dark.

"And you," Light murmured as she stepped up beside Gardina. "This is as much your realm as the world itself. You are half-dead and half-alive. You can call both planes your home. You alone can pass between at will."

Gardina huffed out a quick breath. "It's a lot to take in." She frowned. "Why did Dark never appear to me?"

"You would never have listened to him." She flicked a finger at Gardina's nose. "You are innocent enough to easily believe I was merely a figment. You would have suspected sooner what he is. And, well, he is a much more temperamental sort. He would have scolded you more than once. He has not been without his influence, though. He has been there a few times. He interfered more directly lately when he helped save Matthias from drowning."

"So I *did* see someone. At least I'm not losing my mind entirely."

A smile tugged at Light's lips. "Wait until you are a mother full-time. Sanity will disappear entirely." She brushed a tender kiss over Gardina's forehead. "Return now. You know what must be done. Your story is merely the first. A happy ending waits for others you love as well."

Gardina did not ask. She suspected she already knew. "Thank you." She lifted up off the ground and shimmered as she reached out for the land of the living. Her sight blurred briefly and she found herself back in the Crypt of Kings. It seemed as if nothing had happened at first, then she felt her lover's hands curl warmly around her waist. To her utter surprise, he was able to touch and hold her even though she was still translucent. She could actually feel him as well. "Matt?"

"Who else?" He nuzzled behind her ear. "I had an . . . interesting visitor. He unlocked a few additional gifts related to the moon of my birth rather than the moon of my Runic. Now I can hold you at any time."

She turned in his arms and went solid as she wreathed her arms around his neck. "I'm not sure you want to marry me," she told him solemnly, but with an impish light in her eyes. "I have very strange parents."

"As I get the impression that they *picked* me for you," he retorted dryly, "I find that I don't have any problems." He smoothed her hair out of her face before leaning down and kissing her warmly. "We're running out of nighttime," he murmured. "I think I would prefer to go to the frontlines. I feel like making a big show of things. How long would it take us to get there?"

"We could probably make it right around dawn since you can now fly like normal Etyrnals, but dawn will make your power ineffective."

Pause. Then, "Etyrnals can *fly*?!"

She started grinning. "Oh, didn't I mention that part?" She had to laugh as he swung her around happily, a look of sheer delight on his face. No Etyrnal ever told their Devoted about the best part of being an Etyrnal until after the choice had been made. Humans had tried for ages to fly like the Fae did. Etyrnals kept mum on their ability to fly so that Humans didn't feel more left out. "You're so sweet." She gave him a smacking kiss.

"Can we fly if our power is diminished?"

"Nope."

"Hmm." He frowned thoughtfully as he put her down on her feet. "Let's stay here for the rest of the night and tomorrow, and as soon as the sun sets and I have power again, you can laugh at me while you teach me to fly. We should get to the frontlines by the time the moons fully rise."

"A sound strategy from the Commander of the Armed Forces," she teased. "Or was that the prince talking? Hmmm." She pursed her lips. "You know, I do believe you are the first ruler since Alexander to be as good a warrior as he is a monarch. Other kings and queens were better at ruling and so left battle up to others."

"Maybe we can get rid of the need altogether," he groused. "Or would we need to worry about other lands?"

"If they haven't attacked in the last six hundred years," she noted reasonably, "then they won't attack at all. *Especially* if, you know, the countries are united." Her breath caught as he tugged her close and teasingly nipped at her neck. The little edge of his incisors was wickedly thrilling. "Don't you dare seduce me in here!"

"Why not?"

"I'm not making love with you while a bunch of spirits of your ancestors watch!" she almost wailed. "Don't you *even!*" Her breath whooshed out on a combination of giggles and protest as he tumbled her down onto the floor. She couldn't even go translucent to get away from him since he could hold her now. And, well, she kind of didn't want to get away.

Some sort of power swept through the room and doused the fires along the troughs. Only small, lingering flames shed any light. The majority of the crypt was protectively enfolded within warm shadows and darkness. Most would have had difficulty seeing anything in there, but Etyrnal eyes were highly sensitive—hence sleeping without *any* light at all. Matthias and Gardina could still see each other clearly.

Clothes were shed and used as a bed. Fingers lingered and teased. Teeth nipped just hard enough to draw blood but always healed the mark after. Breathless laughter mixed with sighs. And when physical and emotional need met and overwhelmed them both, even their Runics glowed brightly in response to the pleasure of the moment. In the peaceful aftermath, the torches dimmed entirely to bring the sheltering embrace of the darkness.

Gardina had never felt more alive than she did there, in her lover's arms, in that crypt. Only he could bring her to life. For three centuries, she had existed closer to her half-dead side while only occasionally visiting her half-living side. She felt ready to switch that around. Life was where Matthias resided. She would continue her hunt for it was truly important, but it would be a job and not her entire existence. Her existence was caring for her Devoted on whatever path he chose, and helping to raise an imp of a half-Fae far too much like *either* of her parents than was healthy.

Thinking about it made her fall asleep smiling. She did not dream, not yet, but the promise of it lingered. She slept without stirring even once.

Chapter Sixteen

Gardina woke as the sun was going down and to the feel of lips and hands tenderly caressing her body. She sighed and turned closer to Matthias as his fingers trailed down her Runic mark. "I *really* like a quick learner."

"I'm a big believer in practice making perfect." He kissed her softly and lingered over her flavor for many moments. When they eased back, he murmured huskily, "I like my new senses. It's nearly pitch black in here and yet I can see you."

"That may well be just me." She smiled and skimmed her fingers down his lips. "Remember, you are the one who always can see me. I am both Light and Dark. Neither light nor dark can stop you from seeing me. I can see you relatively well, but I have to work to pick out details. I really, really like taking the effort for it."

Because it was night and his power had returned, they gathered up their clothes and got dressed. Getting blood was a priority since flying could be draining, and Matthias needed a fresh infusion until he was more settled into his power. Gardina could feed him herself, but it was never too early to teach him biting etiquette.

First things first: teaching him how to fly. She bit her lip to hide a laugh as she stayed back a step. "We don't flap our arms or anything. That's silly. Also, we usually nix the cloaks for it or tie them down. Might look flashy, but it creates resistance like you wouldn't believe. You just need to force your power to suspend between you and the ground and push you upward. Power is lighter than air."

"You make it sound simple," he muttered. He blew out a breath and tried to will his power without actually casting it, but all he did was blow out a crater under his feet. He carefully moved away a step and tried again, and this time added a jump as if to increase propulsion. No dice.

She was outright giggling by that point. "I really wish I could help, but there's just no way to explain it. We *all* go through this."

"Even you?"

"Remind me to tell you about the time I got myself stuck on the top of a turret and had to be rescued by Selene."

That made him feel better. He took a breath, centered himself, and reached for his power. He slowly began to rise off the ground without doing damage and opened his eyes carefully. His surprise at seeing himself float promptly ruined his concentration. His power popped like a bubble and sent him flipping head over heels so that he crashed onto the grass in the middle of a new crater.

She rushed to his side to help him, but she was still giggling. "Oh, Matt! I'm so sorry for laughing, but that was priceless!" She helped him up and brushed at the dirt clinging to his clothes. A hint of red had turned his cheeks pink, and it was utterly adorable. She kissed him softly. "Try again."

He would be damned if he took all night to get this right. He blew out a hard breath and reached for his power. Rather than trying to change the way he cast it, as he had been, he merely let it bubble over like a fountain rather than a directional hose. His feet left the ground without any problems, and he discovered he was surprisingly stable. "At the risk of ruining it, I think I got it!"

The boyish, happy smile he sent her made her whole world bright. Becoming an Etyrnal had given him a second childhood to enjoy. Learning and savoring new emotions and experiences and making mistakes toward happiness. She had always found the process endearing, and it was also beautiful inside him. Perhaps because it was the only childhood he had ever been given.

He proved to be, as always, a quick learner. It was only a few minutes before he was flying naturally and safely. It took a great deal of coaxing on her part to get him to a higher altitude, but once he was convinced he wouldn't fall, he followed her into the sky. "Once you turn it on, you have to consciously turn it off," she promised. "It's figuring out the startup that's difficult!"

"If you *dare* tell Niall . . ."

"Oh, he had his share. Also, he really wasn't adjusting to the depth perception change and flew into the side of a building." He perked up at the thought and she shook her head. The two males were incorrigible.

They stopped in the first city they found along their route, and she gave Matthias a lesson in how to hunt safely. The reason why Humans did not remember being bitten was that they were briefly hypnotized by the Etyrnal's power. Whether they had a Runic or not—Greater or not—did not matter. An Etyrnal still drew power from a moon. That power could be used to briefly hypnotize Humans, and some Fae.

"It doesn't hurt them," Gardina explained. "As I

said, there's barely a prick to be felt. *But* it can be emotionally daunting to some. Rather than risk someone panicking and hurting themselves, we block their cognizance of it." She shook her head. "Hurting others is abhorrent to Etyrnals. Didn't you notice you've barely felt your lack of a gun?"

He gently closed the bite he had made on his donor and looked at Gardina in surprise. "I hadn't." Strangely, he felt no desire to be armed at all, and he had spent *years* armed. Until he had become an Etyrnal, he had felt absolutely naked without a gun. Perhaps it was partially because he had far more potent weapons now, but there was indeed a lingering distaste in his mouth at the idea of causing harm to another unless that person was directly harming him or his loved ones first. "Strange how you can go from thinking offensively to defensively," he murmured.

"It's a slight but significant difference. It's why Etyrnals don't become soldiers. It has nothing to do with unfair advantages or a lack of interest in the politics of our chosen lands. It's simply because becoming a soldier basically requires you to get the other guy before he gets you, and we don't want to get him unless he is actively engaging in said getting of us, and even then it gets sketchy." She smiled. "That doesn't mean we don't know *how* to engage in forms of combat. It just means we don't *use* them."

"What would it take to make an Etyrnal voluntarily fight a war?"

"Nothing less than the protection of his or her Devoted. If you had needed it of me, I would have joined the field." She released their donors and sent them on their way none the wiser. She then flew up into the air and waited for Matthias to join her. "I use a sword, in case you were wondering what my weapon of choice is."

"I saw you chopping vegetables that first night. I believe it."

It took only a short two hours to find themselves in Desertia land and approaching the site of the battle. Or rather, the site of the standoff. Matthias was utterly shocked to see that there was absolutely *no* combat occurring. Blood stained the land where battle had once been engaged, but it had completely ceased entirely. In fact, he even saw some of his former soldiers trading supplies with soldiers of the other side. In a murmur, he told Gardina, "I don't mind admitting when I'm wrong. So this is what you meant when you said it was leaders who want war, and not people."

"It can sometimes be the people, but never wholly. Who wants to willingly spill blood? Take life?" She shook her head. "Very few. Dominating natures drive us to try to dominate others, but there are always ways other than war. And this . . . this was not merely a ploy for land. It was the greedy grasp of evil seeking power and destruction. If Feran had somehow found a Runic and become an Etyrnal, he would have immediately become a *nosferatu*."

His head jerked around. "They exist."

"More frequently than we wish," she admitted. "Etyrnals who are driven mad on bloodlust and/or power will corrode and become consumed with the lust for blood. There are punishments for such a thing; the power inside them becomes unstable, for one. A Light Etyrnal would not be able to stand even a smidge of moonlight. Likewise with Darks and the sun. There is no rest for them. They are always awake, always aware, always on the hunt. Vlad hunts them in turn. He has been hunting since he was twelve. He has saved thousands with his efforts."

That sounded like something he needed to know more about later. He put it aside for the time and landed lithely on the edges of his encampment. His entrance was not unnoticed. Several soldiers rushed forward to surround him. He would have tensed but they all immediately saluted. Relief filled all faces. "Welcome back, Commander Logan!" one announced. "We were worried about you when we heard of the bounty!"

Another scowled. "I still don't know why it was placed!" she muttered.

Matthias calmly and deliberately held up his hand and revealed the Runic mark. Silence fell as it was recognized. "As if my entrance had not been a clue," he said calmly, "I am a Dark Etyrnal now. In fact, I am a True Etyrnal. I have claimed the Sovereign Runic as by right of my royal birth. I am Tobias Sovereign, and as the only living member of the royal bloodline, I believe I am your rightful king."

Without any hesitation, every soldier in the vicinity promptly kneeled and bowed their heads. Others who saw the action were quick to follow suit. The wave spread quickly across the camp along with word of what he had claimed. Not a single person was surprised. It truly made sense of many things.

"How do you want to be addressed?" one of his lieutenants asked.

He smiled wryly. "To be honest, I am used to

being called Matthias, and I am choosing to keep that name. The original Matthias Logan was my friend and he saved my life by pretending to be me. I will honor his life by continuing to use his name. For now, if you choose to refer to me as your commander, 'Commander Logan' will suffice. If you choose to address me as your king, 'King Tobias' will do. I can multitask."

More than one person snickered. Several hurried off to spread word, and one soldier saluted as she stood. "What are your first orders, Your Highness?"

Now *that* would take getting used to hearing! He crossed his arms. "Contact the commander of Desertia's forces and offer an immediate ceasefire and peace treaty. Their envoy is invited to our camp to discuss things. There will be no more war." He turned to another. "Focus all resources on healing the wounded, on both sides, and make the supply trade formal. Arrange for the final tally of the dead so that families may be notified."

"I can aid with that," Gardina offered.

It was the first time the others had noticed her hovering right behind Matthias, and several eyes widened. Matthias hid a smile. "This is Gardina

Campbell," he explained. "She is the Gray Etyrnal as well as a crown princess of Coronia. She's also my future wife, and therefore your future queen, and should be treated with the respect you give me. Trust her to know exactly what to do with the dead."

Some soldiers ran off to contact the other side, and others moved to begin the unpleasant but necessary process of assessing the dead. Gardina started to go past Matthias only to stop, turn, and kiss him hotly in front of everyone. A blend of cheers and laughter filled the air. She released him and grinned impishly. "I couldn't resist ruining your intimidating reputation. Sorry."

"Off with you!" he ordered, but he was smiling. As was her way, she had sensed he was more unbalanced than he let on, and she had set out to correct it. He started toward where his tent was still standing, and it was a surreal experience. He had spent a long time there, and in a short few weeks, it had ceased to feel familiar.

He was elbow deep in the neatly stacked reports to find out what had been happening when the bell outside his tent chimed. "Enter," he called.

The flap was pulled back and a soldier walked

in escorting an unfamiliar woman. She stood at a rather short height, yet she looked sleek and dangerous. Her milky pale skin was matched with thick blond hair and pale blue eyes. She wore an envoy's uniform, and a pin affixed to her lapel showed the crest of Desertia. She smiled when she saw him. "Greetings, King Tobias."

He studied her for a moment and smiled. "Just Matthias will do. You are?"

"Riki Fiera." She sketched a bow as the soldier left the tent. "Yes, I am a Dark Etyrnal as well. I volunteered my services as an envoy to Desertia long before the war began. I am glad it has ended. I'm not ashamed to say that I entertained one or two thoughts about smiting King Feran. Even Etyrnals can be pushed to the point of violence if it will protect others."

"*Former* king." He sat back in his chair with a cool smile. "The kingdom is mine now. The people are mine. His life will be mine shortly enough as well. No order he issues will be obeyed."

She sat down across from him with a grin. "I think I like you, Matthias." She propped her chin on her hand. "Then again, I liked you the moment I realized you were Gardina's Devoted, and I liked you even more once I saw you two were of the eternally compatible type."

"I'm a rather likeable sort. Is Desertia interested in alliance rather than war?"

"Indeed! Bickering stepkids though our lands may be, we are tired of the animosity. Our queen has given me full authority to speak on behalf of the country. We would love to put a formal seal on the alliance with a union between families, as Rikan and Coronia will shortly be, but as you will not bear children, I suppose we shall have to take what we are given."

"Don't be so sure," he murmured. "There is as yet a wild card in play. And, actually, I do have a daughter. Adopted, though, so she does not carry Sovereign blood. It's a pity. If she was mine by blood, she would also carry Gardina's Campbell blood."

"I'm not sure that's a pity. It would be a scary combination."

He laughed. "I take it you know Gardina?"

"We've known each other for just shy of thirty years," Gardina announced as she walked into the tent. "She's seventy-three now, if you were wondering how much older she is. Her patron is the Fire Moon."

She smiled at her lover. "While I was doing dead stuff, I also had a missive sent to Selene. I want her and Niall to come here as quickly as possible with Kae. She was nearly killed in the war Feran began. She deserves to see him be defeated. Among other things," she added in a murmur. Louder, she continued, "You might also get a chance to finally meet my cousin. I had to send the missive to Ashfort and that means they were visiting Vlad at his home."

Matthias did not miss the way Riki stiffened slightly. Suspicions began to simmer inside, but he said nothing. "Good to know. On all of it. I admit I'm curious to meet him. You love him a great deal, and I get the feeling he's like a son to you."

She grinned impishly. "He is in some ways, which means you're technically about to be his stepfather, and that'll be funny because he's older than you by like six years." She blew him a kiss. "I have a few more things to do. I'll be back soon."

It did not take long for Riki and Matthias to hammer out the majority of the details of the alliance. It would be drawn up formally and signed off during a ceremony where both he and the queen could be present, but it was considered effective immediately by both sides.

Midnight had crept up by the time Riki left the tent. She would return a copy of the alliance to her queen with the intent of scheduling a meeting when Matthias' coronation had been made official. No doubt Feran was already on his way to the field to engage his usurper. Riki didn't worry about the outcome. It was assured.

"You know," Gardina's voice said idly behind her, "I have a whole new respect for you."

Riki slowly turned around. "How so?"

"Having now had a Devoted of my own, I can see how hard it must be for you to let Vlad do what he is doing."

Her hands slowly curled into fists. "It would destroy his heart and soul if he could not hunt the one who destroyed his family. And if he knew that I was here, that I suffered watching him suffer, he would cease to hunt. I'm damned if I do, and damned if I don't, Ghosty. I love him so damn much."

"What about when he succeeds?" she asked quietly. "We both know he will, Riki. We both know that Nefarin will come after him directly, and Vlad will get him with the gold arrow he has been saving. Nefarin cannot stand to Vlad's will. But what happens when it is done? When the thing Vlad lives for has left his life?"

"I just don't know." Riki lifted her hands helplessly. "He deserves to know he is a Devoted. He, more than any, deserves the gift of eternity."

"Only you can give him that gift."

"I know!" She raked her hands through her hair. "I suppose we shall see how the years go." Longing filled her voice. "I haven't seen him in five years." She bowed gracefully. "Until later, Gardina."

"Indeed." Gardina linked her hands together as she watched the other Etyrnal walk away across the sands. She supposed she ought to have told Riki that Kane had a different obsession than merely gaining vengeance for his family: he wanted just as strongly to find the Etyrnal who had saved his life.

Riki's reaction to him said that there would no doubt be compatible hormones between them. He had the unwavering will and determination to find his answers. Not only would they eventually have to meet, but it would be one hell of an explosion when they did. "Is that also destiny?" she murmured.

Light seemed to ripple across the Fire Moon only then slowly beginning to appear in a sky. A smile tugging at her lips, Gardina headed for Matthias' tent.

That was as good an answer as any. She kinda liked being a believer again. It was much less stressful to know there was *someone* out there keeping an eye on things.

* * * * *

Gardina's message arrived at Kane's cottage the same moment that word of the war's end did. It was only mid-morning the very day after the event had occurred, but word traveled fast on Iria when it needed. The last few days had been interesting for the two Etyrnals and Kane, to say the least. Kae had awakened the afternoon before and was better than new.

Her wings had fully unfurled and allowed her to hover, fly forward, and even upward to some degree. Sadly, backwards and down were not yet within her seven-year-old scope, and she was under strict orders from Niall to not get more than a foot off the ground unless someone was there to catch her. That didn't stop her from fluttering along behind the adults during the day. Perhaps a bit blessedly, she had conked out right at sunset as if she needed to recharge. As much as they loved her, the Etyrnals hoped it would stay. Some peace would be appreciated. Both greatly looked forward to turning her over to her parents.

Kane's limp was barely noticeable as he returned from getting the mail, and he dropped the newspaper on the table in front of Niall. "Ghosty and Matthias have been busy."

Niall quirked a brow and picked up the paper. The headline said it all: *Missing Sovereign Heir has Reclaimed Throne, Declared Peace, and Announced Betrothal to Coronia Crown Princess.* "Jumpin' gophers," he whistled. "That boy's been damn busy, indeed! If he's recognizable as the heir, he must've found and fused the Greater Runic." He skimmed over the article. "Feran's on his way to challenge the veracity of the claim. Ha! He knows it's real."

"He would sooner hope to challenge and defeat Matthias in order to earn right to the Sovereign himself," Selene noted as she sat down beside him. The shift to a diurnal schedule had been difficult but they maintained it for Kae's sake. They could rest when their duty was done.

"You know," Kane said slowly, "that bothers me. Why in the name of the gods would Feran even possibly think he has any chance to defeat Matthias?

Matthias already had age, skill, and health on him. The Runic will have enhanced all of that, and he is backed by the Gray Etyrnal's power. Feran has a . . . trump of some sort."

Kae fluttered into the room and very nearly bumped into the table since her ability to stop was also still growing. Niall was quick enough to catch her, thankfully. He put her down on her chair. "You *will* have to use your feet, little mite."

"Mommy doesn't." She had ceased to call Gardina anything but the title she wanted her to be. As far as she was concerned, it was just a matter of time until she got both the parents she wanted.

"She does, too." He tugged on her pigtail. "She walks often enough that she doesn't forget how. For every room y'cross on wing, you have to cross 'nother on foot. Deal?"

"Deal!" She propped her chin on her hands. "What's in the paper that has you guys excited?"

"Your father has become a Dark Etyrnal and a king," Selene offered with a hint of dryness. "He's formally announced he's marrying your mother, and he's ended the war that brought you into his life."

Kane put down the letter he had been holding.

"Gardina wants us to travel there and see the official end when Matthias achieves justice for his family—all of it. They expect Feran to be there sometime tonight."

"Why wouldn't he wait until Daddy was weak by the day?" Kae asked reasonably.

"Laws of succession. He has to challenge the heir's right to the throne within forty-eight hours or it is decreed binding. If Matthias did not bear the Greater Sovereign Runic, he would have to prove himself within that same time. He has proven himself. Now Feran must challenge it. Matthias was quite clever to time things the way he did. Or perhaps Gardina guided him." Selene got to her feet. "I suppose we had best set out now. If we get some very fast horses, we can make it an hour or two after sundown."

"Wish we could fly," Niall groused.

"No thanks. Not after you dropped me the last time," Kane groused back.

Selene just sighed. "March! We have precious little time left. We will have to find a way to wake Kae after sundown. Perhaps Gardina can help with that. She is both Light and Dark. A boost of Light power might stretch Kae's endurance."

"Reckon it's time *that* got explained as well,"

Niall murmured.

Kane smiled. "Reckon so."

Chapter Seventeen

The day had been busy at the encampment as well. The blistering heat had been helpfully alleviated on the Rikan side by members of Desertia showing them how to use Water Runics to bring the temperature down even a few degrees to where it would be tolerable. Matthias' tent had been heavily reinforced to block out the sunshine, and he slept deeply to prepare for the battle he knew loomed ahead. He, too, suspected Feran may have a few tricks. Soldiers stood guard outside his tent while Gardina drifted in and out. She had taken over leadership duties, as was her right as future queen.

She was in the middle of overseeing the start of dismantling the encampment when a soldier approached. He saluted and she smiled. "Yes?"

"My lady . . . I wonder if you might answer a question?"

"Sure."

"General Richards."

He didn't say more than that, but she understood anyway. "He is not a concern. When I last saw him, he was . . . conflicted. He has been losing control of his body and mind to an invasive presence I could not help him with." She made a vague gesture. "When we see him again, he will not be who he used to be. The body may belong to Darren Richards, but the mind and soul will be different."

Sensing he would get no more answers if he asked, he instead saluted and went on his way. She continued on with her work and found herself actually enjoying it. Maybe it was the royal blood inside her. And here Niall had always said she was just bossy.

As the sun was beginning to finally set, she returned to her sleeping lover's side and gently coaxed him awake. She had fed more than needed from a few willing soldiers so that she could provide for Matthias. She didn't think he would be comfortable biting any of his soldiers—she had no such compunctions—and by the blood being processed first by her body, it would make him stronger.

It was only the presence of the guards outside the rather thin walls that made him keep his hands to himself while he fed. Control was slowly arriving, but it was slow going. He mostly blamed her. He didn't think there was supposed to even be control between them. Once fed and his power returned, they headed out of the tent into the night.

Less than an hour later, the thunder of hooves had them turning to discover riders had arrived. Matthias recognized Selene and Niall, and he could make an educated guess as to the identity of the large man. It was confirmed when Gardina positively brightened and rushed forward to hug him tightly. "Vlad!" She clung onto his neck. "I've missed you!"

He hugged her back with a smile. The striking contrast they made between their literal negative images had more than one person wishing they knew how to paint, Matthias included. Kane looked over to assess the man who was his mother's Devoted and decided he liked everything he saw. "It's an honor," he said softly and sincerely.

Matthias bowed. "Likewise, Kane. I assume that is your preference? I noticed only Gardina has called you Vlad."

"It is my preference, and she's the only one I let get away with using my first name." He sighed as he dismounted. "The horses are spent. We pushed them far, far too hard to be here in time."

Matthias glanced to a soldier. "Tend to them." He crooked a brow as

Selene and Niall approached as well, and he noticed that Kae was wrapped up in a cloak as she slept against Niall's shoulder. "Well, someone's tired."

"Was out as soon as the sun set," Niall confirmed. "Been doin' that since her wings broke in."

"Wings!" He winced. "That's a whole new genre of child-proofing." He took his daughter and cuddled her close. The warm feel of her snuggling against him was a different level of contentment. He didn't even notice the way he relaxed more, though other sharp eyes did. They all smiled.

"Feran is due here within the next two hours," Gardina offered to the newcomers. "I suppose we could let Kae sleep until then, but best she be up now and take in the area first." She moved closer and lightly bit her wrist until gray blood welled. She pressed her wrist to Kae's mouth and coaxed softly, "Wake and take my power, fledgling. You know you need it."

Lashes fluttered slightly though did not lift. She did drink though, and the cycle of Light inside the Ghost Runic shortly had her stirring. When she realized who was holding her, she let out a squeal of delight and grabbed onto him happily. "Daddy!"

He had to laugh. "I missed you too!" He looked

at the gathered crowd and lifted a brow. "This child is my adopted daughter, Kaeleigh. She is your princess. She is half-Fae and half-Human." He gingerly unwrapped her from the cloak and her wings unfurled. They were a beautiful, shimmery blue water color that offset her vibrant red hair. "I expect you to protect her with your lives if it is needed."

"Yes, sir!" came the chorus of responses.

Kae looked at Gardina and asked hopefully, "Mommy?"

She held her arms for an answer and cuddled the little girl close when she flew right into her arms. "You could still call me Ghosty."

"Nope. You're Mommy now." She held onto the Etyrnal's neck happily. She had gotten just about everything she had ever wanted. Now they just had to get rid of that icky old king and it would be perfect.

"Hey, you want to meet the person who saved you?" Matthias asked softly. "His name is Jerrod. I bet he would be glad to see you're alive. He risked a lot by bringing you to me, and he kept my departure a secret. He could have been executed for it."

She nodded enthusiastically. "I want to thank him!"

Gardina obligingly carried her into camp, and

every soldier they passed watched them with awe. Either alone was striking enough, but mother and daughter together were almost too ethereal to look at. Matthias predicted Kae having the army eating out of her hand within the next hour; they already looked a bit smitten.

He spotted Snacks trotting in the wake of his family and pinched the bridge of his nose. "Would someone like to explain how my kid got wings and I ended up with a grumbler for a pet?"

Niall laughed and clapped him on the back. "Let's grab a drink, fledglin', and I'll be glad to explain. I reckon you've got a few interestin' tales of your own."

"That's one word for it."

It did not take long to have everyone on the same page. They had already been piecing together each other's stories, and Matthias did not resent Selene for keeping her silence on his identity. He wasn't sure he would have been able to handle it at the start of things. There was still the question of Feran, of course, and the last mystery about Kae to be revealed. Matthias would have already made the announcement, but he wanted Feran there to find out just how badly he had lost.

While Niall and Kane entertained Kae, Matthias began to prepare for the coming battle. He intended to don his old armor, but he was surprised when a soldier opened the tent flap and announced, "Commander, we have something that was fetched as soon as you announced your identity." She moved back to let in others carrying a trunk. "It is rightfully yours."

Understandably puzzled, he knelt beside the trunk and found it sealed with a lock that only the Sovereign could release. He did so, and Gardina helped him heft the heavy lid open; it weighed a damn ton. His jaw dropped as he beheld what lay inside the trunk, and even Gardina's brows shot up.

The glimmering, gleaming red armor glowed as brightly as the Runic itself. It had been forged and crafted by a master, and it had been designed to be worn by a warrior king or queen. It was perhaps the most spectacular piece of workmanship he had ever seen. With it came a sword that had a blade the same red as the armor, and a hilt carved from wood and crystal. The family crest of the royal line was engraved into the place where blade met hilt.

"Nostalgia," Gardina murmured. "Remember

me saying you were the first warrior king since Alexander? Guess who wore this last."

"Amazing." He let out a long breath. "This looks like a two person job to be put on. Am I supposed to have a squire or something? I'm new to this king thing."

She giggled. "Well, yes, you could, but usually a monarch is aided by his or her significant other. It's for good luck. Sort of an 'I put you in it, so you have to come home safe where I can take you out of it' kind of thing." She trailed her fingers over the metal. "It must have burned Feran," she murmured, "to be unable to claim many 'rightful' things he earned as being king. There are no doubt others sealed by the Sovereign to be used only by you."

"Why would they be sealed if they didn't expect this to happen?"

"Safety measure to prevent them from theft." She began to pull out pieces and put them aside. "You know what the bright side about this is?"

"What?"

"You absolutely took care of the problem of not being promoted to general by being promoted to king."

It made him smile, as she had intended. "I'm a

big believer in finding the best person for the job."

She helped him don each piece in turn and deliberately added protective symbols branded from her Ghost Runic. The nice thing about being Gray was that she could bolster and empower both other kinds of her brethren. She was also not ashamed to admit that her lover looked really, really, sexy in the armor. It was flattering in some ways, and it emphasized his inner strength as well as his outer. She very much looked forward to the 'taking him out of the armor' part.

He was fully armored and prepared for battle not long before the shout went up that there was a party approaching. He calmly sheathed his sword at his side and ducked out of the tent. Gardina was at his side as he moved toward the edge of the encampment, and he noticed when Selene and Kane fell into step behind them. Niall lingered at the edges, a lethal new gun visible on his hip. Kae stood in front of him and had wrapped his cloak around herself. Her eyes were calm.

The party was a very small handful of soldiers who actually followed Feran faithfully, Feran himself, and Darren. That this was all Feran had mustered to join him in challenging Matthias was a telling thing.

Matthias looked at Darren sharply and knew immediately that Gardina had been correct: Darren Richards was no more. His aura wavered brighter than before, and his eyes had shifted from their normal blue to an interesting pale purple. Eyes were the window to the soul. The quickest way to determine possession was to see if the eyes changed color.

With a calm that was bone-deep, Matthias said, "You'll forgive me if I don't kneel. I serve no false king."

Hatred glittered out of Feran's mad eyes. Only one held sight any longer. The other had been wholly blinded by the gray blood that had seared through to the bone. "I should have killed you as soon as I discovered the Gray Etyrnal hovering near you."

"And then you would have been doomed to damnation sooner rather than later," came Gardina's surprisingly cool retort. "Had even a hair been out of place, I would have rent your life in two."

A visible chill rippled down his skin. He dismissed her and looked at Matthias again. "How did you find the Sovereign Runic? Where had it been hidden? I have searched for thirty years!" he screamed. "How did I never find it?!"

"It was under your nose all the time." Matthias inclined his head. "It would seem that in the escape, the Sovereign was placed inside me for safety. It was there all along. It revealed itself at the moment when I most wanted to live. On the verge of drowning, it was there to save me."

A brief shocked moment followed his words. Feran jerked toward Gardina. "You knew!" he raged. "You lied! When I questioned you, you knew all along where it was!"

"Okay, seriously, you expected me to tell you the truth? You couldn't kill me. I had nothing to lose. Yeah, it hurt to be abused to within an inch of my half-dead side, but it was all healable." She ignored the spreading distaste at the knowledge that she had been tortured. Even in the midst of war, no higher crimes existed than torture and rape. "And, actually, you were kinda screwed more than you think. The entire time I was there, *I* had the Sovereign Runic." She touched her mark. "I was carrying it inside my Runic. It was right under your nose!"

In a voice no less chilly, in a tone that could only be called regal, Matthias added, "You also screwed up in another way, Feran. Do tell me. Why were you interested in the half-Fae I rescued?"

Feran's breaths came hard and fast as his lungs struggled for air under the pressure of his fury and loathing. "I suspected she might be connected to the Vargas royal family of Desertia and therefore useable to gain the Greater Water Runic. The crown prince married a Fae. Rumor said they managed to have a child. When she survived the impossible, I thought she might be that child."

Niall scooped up Kae and walked forward to put her gently on the ground in front of Matthias. He remained kneeling by her side for support, and her small hand sought his for comfort. She knew her Uncle Niall and her father would keep away the bad people. Matthias lightly touched her hair soothingly. "You are correct. Meet Kaeleigh Logan, formerly Kaeleigh Vargas. She is the firstborn child of the late crown prince of Desertia, and therefore she has a direct claim to the throne. She is their crown princess, should she wish it."

That Kae would not know her own heritage despite her age was not surprising. Unlike Humans who could remember back to the age of two, Fae could only remember back to the age of five. Her earliest memory dated to just after her father had abdicated. If neither he nor his wife had ever mentioned it, Kae had no way of knowing. And by her family mark changing to the one of her foster family, her identity had been lost entirely . . . except for one thing.

"You want to know how we knew who she is?" Matthias asked. "It was a few things. For one, her pupils bear the blue hue that means she is influenced by the Greater Water Runic, and only the Vargas family would have that. For two, the timing. She lost her parents around the same time that the crown prince and his wife died. And for three . . . well, perhaps we had best show you."

He knelt beside his daughter and gently pressed his Runic hand to the still-changing family mark on her arm. It had mostly faded to leave only residue behind, and it looked much like his barren mark did. Their family had not fully formed, not yet. A blue glow began to emanate from her skin and a small blue sphere emerged from the center of the lingering mark only to fall into his palm. The symbol inside glowed brightly.

A murmur rippled through the entire crowd as they realized what they were looking upon. Very calmly, Gardina said, "It is all speculation, since Kae would be the only who knows, and she has no memory of that age, but I think that she may have accidentally come upon the Runic and it chose her as its master. At that age, she could not fuse a Runic of any sort. You can only take a Runic from age six and up. But since she had no knowledge of it, it stayed dormant inside her."

"A half-Fae who can use a Greater Runic." Niall smirked at a gaping Feran. "She's likely the rarest creature on t'planet, second only to her mama for power." He looked at Kae very solemnly. "It's your choice, little mite. Y'wanna hand over the Runic to Feran, or do you wanna keep it? If y'fuse it now, you'll be the littlest Etyrnal on the block."

Remembering Dark's words, Matthias was not at all surprised when Kae reached out and took the Runic from him with her right hand. Though not as prepared as he had been, she was just close enough to being a Devoted that the process went relatively quickly and painlessly. She passed out almost immediately into his arms. He gave her to Niall who bundled her up safely in his cloak once more. She was a Light Etyrnal now, and at her age, the moonlight would be too much for her delicate skin to endure.

A low rumble began to well up inside Feran until it became an enraged roar that split the sky. The sound was chilling and disturbing to even Gardina and Kane who had seen their share of evil. The roar turned into agonized coughing that sent him tumbling out of the saddle and onto the floor in an undignified heap. Blood dripped from his lips as he shoved himself up to his feet. An odd glow rippled over his body, and he seemed to take in strength.

Kane realized it first. "He has Runics embedded all over his body to prolong his life." He drew the crossbow on his hip and fired it fast. The bolt tore through Feran's tunic sleeve and ripped away a chunk of material. The globes of glass buried in his flesh glowed brightly and revealed the oozing wounds around where they had been attached. Kane made a disgusted noise. "And some particularly snide people call Etyrnals undead. Here is your undead. He should have died years ago."

With the mania of the damned, Feran lunged toward Matthias. The true king merely held his ground until the last moment and then stepped aside. Feran stumbled past and tripped over his own cloak. He planted face first into the sand. He painfully staggered up to his feet and grabbed for the magic he possessed. He released it as a wave at Matthias that promised to tear him apart.

It merely splashed harmlessly off the breastplate of the armor. Feran's good eye stared blearily at the scene before he collapsed to his hands and knees. Runics began to pop free and roll across the ground. Matthias calmly walked closer and pressed the edge of his sword against Feran's neck. "I have every right to take your life here. You murdered one part of my family and tried to kill the other." He sheathed his sword. "I don't feel that charitable. You're going to spend the last few days of your life in the dungeon where you can revisit your failures as you rot away." He looked at his soldiers. "Take Feran, the former general, and Feran's men captive. Richards and the men can be given the option of swearing fealty and being released or they can join Feran in the dungeon."

The men were not stupid. They chose to swear fealty. They had not believed that Matthias was the rightful heir. They believed it now. Darren said very little at all, and he was therefore arrested. Matthias felt a bit like a huge weight had been lifted from his chest that he had not known was there. "I feel as if I've just fulfilled a promise," he murmured to Gardina as she joined him to watch the two prisoners be escorted away.

"I suppose in a way, you have." She rose up to wind her arms around his neck, and she kissed him softly. A few hoots and hollers in the background made her smile against his lips. "They're easily entertained." She landed and turned when Niall approached. "Gimme." She held out her arms demandingly.

He obligingly handed over the sleeping Kae, and Gardina snuggled her close. Matthias tugged them both close and closed his eyes as an odd feeling swelled inside. Happiness. He wasn't sure he had ever felt that either. Just another gift from his beautiful Gray Etyrnal. He looked forward to spending eternity repaying the favor.

Feran was thrown into the deepest dungeon in the castle. They left him in his elaborate robes and cloak, and they even left him his crown. It wasn't really the proper piece for the king anyway. The true mark of a Sovereign king or queen had been stolen after the coup and hidden away.

The former site of battle had been entirely cleared. The dead had been returned to their families for honorable burial, and those without families had been buried at the site, as was custom. The coronation ceremony was pending for a number of reasons. The surprisingly warmer castle needed a thorough scrubbing to remove all remnants of the former ruler, and the royal chambers especially needed to be redone. They were stripping back to the bare stone and building anew lest bad memories linger.

The other reason was that no one was entirely sure if Matthias actually intended to rule. He had every right to formally abdicate and appoint a new ruling family. Etyrnals tended to avoid society because it was easy to get attached to things that would disappear with time, but some did live quite happily among societies. He had not said one way or another, and not even Gardina knew for sure.

Kae had converted just fine to becoming a True Light Etyrnal. She was still growing and maturing at a normal rate and would not actually achieve eternity until she reached her final peak of maturity. For Humans, it was usually close to forty. For Fae, it was closer to sixty since their natural lifespan was twice as long. Hers could fall anywhere in the middle.

She was slowly adjusting to her new gifts. She still conked out the minute the sun went down, and she was promptly awake with the first hint of dawn. It made things a bit on the interesting side for her parents since Matthias had a tendency to do the exact opposite; he was still adjusting too! Gardina kept Kae's schedule for the time being so that someone was there to watch over her.

Once Kae adjusted, they would both go onto the nocturnal schedule. Gardina had tested a theory and proven that she could effectively create a way for an Etyrnal to rest even when their celestial body was in the sky. It meant Kae would not actually get to use her powers until she was old enough to care for herself during the day, but that might prove to be advantageous. By the time she was out on her own, she would have a control and adaptability that few other Etyrnals might ever have. She would be a Runic Master of a Greater Runic; her limitations would be nearly non-existent.

The happy, cheerful manner and mood had permeated the entire castle. It drifted down to where Feran sat in his cell and fought to ignore the feel of Death breathing down his neck. Everything hurt. He could barely breathe. Torture was knowing each breath might be your last but not yet dying. If they had given him anything to use for a weapon, he would have already killed himself. He would rot away in that disgusting dungeon in his crown and robes. No greater indignity existed.

A footstep had him slowly looking at the cell doors. Shock widened his good eye as he saw Darren negligently leaning against the bars. The former general had been tossed into another dungeon and yet here he stood. "You," Feran rasped. "Get me out of here! I will not die like rotting garbage!"

"Tsk tsk." The voice was not wholly Darren's either, much as the eyes were not. "Such a waste to see such a formerly great man reduced to whining. Rotting like garbage is the least of what you deserve, but it takes far too long. You might languish here for another month, and I'm bored of waiting for it. I'd sooner see the deed done now. I'd say justice will be served in the Evermore." He lifted a hand and pale lavender power flowed over his fingers with a hint of rose petals and green leaves. "So ends the false king."

Feran's mouth opened but nothing emerged except a strangled gurgle as his heart ruptured inside his chest and his lungs shut down. He was dead even before his body hit the floor. Rats scuttled forward to sniff at his boots and then recoiled. Even the scavengers could not bear his tainted evil.

Darren stared down at him for a moment with a smirk and turned to leave. Much to his surprise, a familiar figure was leaning against another cell door. Gardina slowly lifted a brow at him. "You may as well release Richards from your hold. You don't need him anymore."

A lavender glow rippled around his body as he dropped flat to the ground. Left behind was a pale, insubstantial figure that could have been mistaken for a ghost except for the obvious shimmer that threaded through his form. That shimmer marked him as being a spirit that still had a living body.

He had also retained a great deal of his appearance, and his was not an unfamiliar face to Gardina. The long pointed ears on his head and the presence of wings on his back marked him as being wholly of Fae blood. He inclined his head regally at Gardina and said, "When did you peg me?" His natural voice carried a softer and strangely sweeter note than any Human or Etyrnal's might. Another hallmark of his Fae blood.

"Hmm." She tapped a finger on her lips. "To be honest, signs were there from the get-go, but I didn't know until Richards asked me about the 'something' inside him. When did you decide to use him?"

"When I saw Kaeleigh taken in by Matthias." He shrugged. "I knew Richards would be a useful pawn eventually. I killed his body and then forced it to continue to live so that I could take over whenever I needed. I figured he was no loss. He was almost as rotten as Feran."

"Hey, I ain't complainin', as Niall might say." She cocked her head. "Thanks for starting your takeover in time to make him save me from more abuse."

His shrug that time carried discomfort. "It was wrong." Under his breath, he muttered, "Kaeleigh wanted me to help you."

"Oh ho!" She grinned. "You were multitasking. You'd leave Richards to some of his own devices while you looked in on Kae." She pursed her lips. "Do tell why you're interested in my daughter."

"I need a woman who is of Fae blood but a True Etyrnal."

"Ooh, yeah, that does kind of narrow things down to just her. Fae can't use Runics, and half-Fae are really freaking rare without needing one who is connected to a *Greater* Runic." Hello, destiny, she thought with humor. How had she ever thought it didn't exist? "Must've made your century when you realized who and what she is."

"So to speak."

"She's only seven." It was said gently. "The earliest she will possibly be able to help you is the age of twenty, when she can leave home. Whatever you need her to do will have to wait at least that long. I'm afraid you're going to have to learn some patience, Tiernan."

He eyed her for a moment. "Only the Gray Etyrnal would dare mock the prince of the Fae."

"Only the prince of the Fae would dare try to interfere with the Gray Etyrnal's family," was the sweet retort. "Kae will remain with me and her father until she is an adult. Any attempt by you to change things otherwise will be met with swift retaliation. I can pass through Life and Death. I can find you in the place between and make sure you stay there for a *long* time more. Are we clear?"

He seethed for a moment before finally sighing. "Yes ma'am." On a last glower, he disappeared with a shimmer of lavender light.

She wandered over Richards' body and looked down at him. She looked at Feran. She calmly drew out her logbook and flipped back to the page where she had first seen Richards' name. She drew her finger across the *Unconfirmed* and it changed to *Deceased.* With a little flourish, she snapped the book closed and put it away. Things were done. The past was done. Only the future remained.

A smile tugged at her lips. Maybe she ought to tell Kae the bedtime tale of a Fae prince who had offended the wrong Etyrnal and gotten himself cursed for his efforts. It might be amusing to plant the seeds.

Epilogue

Word spread quickly that Feran and Darren were both dead. The official story was that Feran had used the last of his power to kill Darren and then had a heart attack and died as well. Matthias was a bit skeptical over that, but he could get no direct answers from his lover. If she knew something, she was keeping it silent. He didn't really care either way; it was enough to know it was done.

A week to the day after Feran's death, the remodeling was completed. Matthias was given the go-ahead that he could move into the royal chambers . . . if he wanted. He and Gardina had been staying in a different suite entirely while the work was being done. Moving or not moving into the royal chambers would signify his decision.

Both he and Kae had adjusted enough to their new selves that he didn't immediately fall asleep with the sun and she didn't immediately fall asleep with the moons. She was slowly acclimating to the nocturnal schedule and would be trying an entire day of sleeping very soon. Gardina had already transitioned, and it was Kane who briefly watched over Kae during the daylight hours she still remained awake.

If the royal family would continue to remain the royal family, the royal chambers needed the finishing touches that would make it suitable for two Etyrnals to rest within. The chambers rightfully belonging to a prince or princess would need the same touches for Kae.

Matthias was standing in the throne room studying the thrones when he felt slender arms curl around his neck. He lightly covered her hands and smiled. "I'm not sure what you'd do if you couldn't hover anymore and do that."

"Be terribly sad. I like hugging you, and you're too tall otherwise." Gardina rested her chin on his shoulder. She freed one of her hands and lightly covered the as-yet barren place where his family mark belonged. "You know we support you either way. I'm already guilty of getting attached to people and places, so, meh. No biggie if it keeps happening. Kae won't need to worry about that for ages, and odds are she won't rule any of the kingdoms she now can claim."

"A hunch?"

"So to speak."

"Hmm." He continued to study the thrones. "After thirty years as a commoner, even the Commander of the Armed Forces, it should be more daunting to realize I am a king. Maybe it's your fault."

"Mine!"

"Hey, you're a crown princess. I had accepted that marrying you would make me a prince-by-proxy long before I knew I was already one. It was always in my mind that you could someday decide you wanted to rule Coronia. And I was okay with that." He began to slowly walk across the room. "I'm okay with the idea that Sovereign blood belongs on the throne. The country needs it, and I love my country. I'm okay with the idea that maybe, just maybe, your parents set all of this up so that the three countries are unified by a family. Okay with the idea that our daughter is effectively the crown princess to all three lands should she wish it. Okay with the fact that all three countries accept that fact, and that your many-greats-nephew and Kae's grandmother have already said that they defer to the right of firstborn without any quibbles."

She released him and smiled as he slowly sat down on the throne. "Is it okay?" she teased.

He tugged her down onto his lap and buried his face in her hair. "It's better than okay. I think it's almost perfect. It will be actually perfect once we move into the chamber, get married, and hope our kid can sleep through an entire day."

She started giggling. "They say new parents don't get a lot of sleep. I guess it's true even for Etyrnals!"

The moment he requested that their things be moved, plans were rushed forward for his coronation ceremony as well as their wedding. The two would be combined together—which wasn't entirely unusual—and right after would be the formal signing of the alliance. It had been expanded to include Coronia, officially, and the royal families of both countries would be traveling out for it. Gardina had authority to sign for Coronia, but she insisted her nephew do it. He ran the country, he could sign the darned paperwork!

The ceremony proved to be beautiful, and a happy Gardina got to wear the wedding dress she had left packed away in the Coronia castle. She thought it fitting that she wear the gown originally meant to carry her down the aisle to another Sovereign prince. The fact that she looked forward to him getting her out of it again told her that she finally had the *right* Sovereign prince.

The entire thing took place at night, of course, and Kae was up and running around as if the moons didn't bother her. She couldn't go outside without covering up entirely, but Selene had made her a special hooded cloak that protected her tender skin from even a hint of moonlight. Laughter filled every corner of the Rikan castle and erased even the last lingering hints of the horror that had once occurred.

Other changes were also being made. The royal crest needed to be updated to match the new symbol of the ruling family. The mark had revealed itself from the moment Matthias and Gardina formalized their vows and became one. On Kae's upper arm, his lower, and Gardina's back shoulder, the symbol had made itself obvious: blended into one were the symbols of the Sovereign, Ghost, and Water Runics. It could be mistaken for nothing else. The moons themselves—the gods themselves—had given their blessing to the new family.

Once the alliance was formally signed off, a copy of it was flown from the highest flagpole, as was custom. It would fly there for a month, as it would over the other two castles. It was considered good luck for all involved. The whole night seemed to speed by until dawn began to subtly hint it was close to rising.

People reluctantly began to disperse home. A finally sleepy Kae was collected by Niall who winked at Gardina as he went by. "I've got the mite. You better enjoy your weddin' night while it's still night, Your Majesty."

She briefly stuck her tongue out at him but grinned as she headed over to her husband. He caught her in his arms to lift her off her feet. "We have about three hours until the sun demands slumber. Let's enjoy them. And make Niall babysit our kid tomorrow night. Maybe the night after."

She giggled and held on as he carried her through the castle toward their chambers. "They can spare their king and queen a few nights, at the least. William's good at keeping an eye on stuff while we're asleep."

Much to their mutual delight, William had proven to be alive and well. He had been reinstated as head of the castle household, and he had full authority to make minor decisions for Matthias and Gardina if they were resting. It made things even easier for the new king and queen.

The chambers were ready and waiting for

them. A fire crackled cheerfully for light and warmth, and the shield stood nearby to cut off the light when it was time for rest. The windows were already wholly shuttered, and the covers had been turned back on the massive bed. Matthias dropped Gardina onto the top and she started laughing as she sank rather than bounce. "I told you it was the springs and not the fluff!"

He tugged her up and deftly started unlacing her bodice. "I admit that jumping on a bed has its merits, but there's something to be said for the way the fluff makes you snuggle against me." He gingerly removed her dress and put it aside. Underneath was nothing except soft, translucent skin that glowed with a hint of gold in the light of the fire. He stopped breathing for a moment. "It's a good thing I didn't know what you didn't have on under there," he managed to say.

She sat up and started tugging at his velvet vest. "You're overdressed, Your Highness." She nipped teasingly at his neck. "Let's enjoy the rest of our night. I don't want to be anywhere but here."

It was sometime later as the first rays of dawn were peeking over the horizon that he thought to ask, "Nowhere but here, huh?" He smoothed her tangled white hair out of her face. She was snuggled into his arms where she belonged. "You don't miss your manor?"

"Hmm, a bit. I'm thinking we ought to rebuild it if only to give us a vacation spot." She wrapped an arm around his waist and sighed happily. "Guess it's the royal blood in me. I'm fond of castles. You helped me reconnect with the living, Matt. It's a gift I can't repay."

"Sure you can." He kissed her lightly. "You can spend eternity teaching me all the stuff I never learned. I even know where to start."

"Hmm?"

"Swimming lessons."

It made her start giggling, as he had hoped. Content with their lives, they put out the fire's light and snuggled down for rest. And this time, for the first, she truly did rest. Both of her loved ones were bound to her as family, and it was their power that finally sheltered her. His Dark turned away the moons even as Kae's Light turned away the sun, and Gardina could finally be weakened enough to dream. She could finally rest.

Eternity was no longer only a dream away. It

had finally arrived.